The
World
or
Nothing

A novel by Amin Sidialicherif

"After a while, you could get used to anything."

-Albert Camus, The Stranger

AUTHOR'S NOTE

When I started writing this book, I desperately wanted to create a story that I would be proud to look back on for the rest of my life. I wanted to capture nostalgia, destiny, tragedy, passion and love in one book. I wanted the emotions that I have felt as a teenager to live on forever. I wanted to instigate emotions as strong as the ones I felt producing it. This book, although about a specific character and plot, was designed to be open-ended and vague. Everything should be taken metaphorically, and everyone is meant to have their own experience reading it.

I hope that you find a deeper meaning in the next these pages, whether it be about fate, psychology, perspective, forgiveness or reflection.

I hope you take something profound away from what I have written.

Most of all, I hope you can apply whatever that is to your own life, your own dimension and ultimately your own destiny.

MUSIC

For optimal experience, it is recommended that the reader listens to music while reading this text. There are 27 songs cited in the book, and it is heavily encouraged that the reader listens to the tracks as they are presented in the story. For more suggested listening while reading, contact the author.

In addition to music, many real-world events, individuals and places are mentioned in the text. The author heavily encourages that readers briefly research any terms they are unfamiliar with.

TIMELINE

This story is written from the perspective of Zinedine Zenoud, a French-born Algerian man born on May 9, 2001. This book is a compilation of his personal journals his adolescence and early adult life.

Throughout the story, our real world's timeline and Zinedine's world's timeline split more and more. If you are reading this novel years after its release, you may notice factual fallacies regarding the 2020's. This is due to the fact that this story takes place in a different dimension and on a different timeline than ours. Many experts have attempted to contemplate the multiverse theory and variations of it for decades. Essentially, the many-worlds interpretation of quantum mechanics states that for every possibility in the history of the universe, a new universe is created in which that possibility takes place. While our world exists on one of those infinite timelines, Zinedine's extremely similar but ultimately different reality exists on another.

The world in which this story takes place is very similar to the one you call home—albeit with slight deviations. In this universe, the 2004 Madrid Train Bombings that claimed the lives of nearly 200 people never happened. Instead, a tag-team duo of French-born Algerian terrorists, trained by Al-Qaeda in Afghanistan, committed mass shootings and eventually suicide bombings in Paris, murdering 314 people. Due to this, the universe in which Zinedine lives has extremes that are a complete contrast to what we know as normal.

This book is dedicated to

Lucas Connor Beirer *(2003-2019)*

Table of Contents

Chapter 1: Sur Paname: April 30, 2017

My neighborhood isn't exactly one that most wanna hang around. The scenery around Barbès isn't something that those American tourists are going to see on their postcards of Paris. It's drab, dark, dry and unsafe at night. It's full of African immigrants. It's somewhere most French Parisians wouldn't walk during the day, let alone once the sun sets. Regardless, it's home. It's all I've known, and it's all I truly remember from my 16 years on this planet. Do I wish this was the case? Not entirely, but in my religion, we believe in fate. We are of the belief that all of time has already been predetermined, and that we are subject to the manifestation of that destiny. And so, because of that destiny, I lie here in Barbés. I sit in my school with half-broken headphones nestled under my hood listening to melancholy cloud rap, considering that I was always meant to be here.

Ibrahim and Wissam, two of my closest friends, are usually alongside me in class. We play soccer together, as we always have. Unfortunately, though, over the years we've been drifting farther and farther apart.

Our parents all come from a region known as the Maghreb. Ibrahim's parents come from Morocco, Wissam's from Tunisia, and mine from Algeria. There are reportedly 6 million Maghrebins in France, but I know the real number is likely much greater considering the vast amount of Maghrebins in Barbès that are illegal. My grandparents were illegal, and later my parents were too.

We have always dreamed of being professional soccer players. We've grown up playing in the streets, playing with our friends, playing with our family. Ibrahim and Wissam have breathtaking amounts of talent—much more than me—but it has gone to waste. The two were in top youth soccer academies but were soon dropped due to their unprofessional tendencies. So here they are again, back in our English lesson, back in the neighborhood, looking faded and angry, as they usually do nowadays.

We immigrants always blame our misfortune on the racism here in France. It's extreme. It's discrimination unlike anything you have ever seen. Because of it, all three of us sit here in this classroom in the hood. It is our destiny. We weren't going to become footballers, even if I was named after the great Zinedine Zidane, whose parents settled in Barbès, and who was a son of Algerian immigrants just as I am. We weren't going to become footballers because we didn't have the courage or confidence to overcome the obstacles in front of us. I was destined to remain in the hood forever. That story was written far before I could understand it, far before I was adopted by my grandfather Yassine, even before my parents were radicalized to the point of no return.

I walk home at the end of my school day, exhausted, and greet my grandpa with the traditional "*Salam U Alaikum*", Arabic for "Peace be upon you". Sometimes I think of asking my grandfather about my parents, but I know it would do more harm than good. It's all on the Internet, page after page, video after video, comment after comment. I know the whole story and asking him would do nothing but worsen the situation. I don't want to induce further despair. He's done so much for me; he saved me from foster care. Being a 2-year-old orphan whose parents had died, it seemed certain I would find myself waiting for adoption. The only reason I was able to go home after my parents committed the atrocities that they did was because my grandpa took me under his wing. He saw those foster homes and knew how I would be treated. He foresaw the discrimination I would feel and knew that that I'd be reminded every day of the fact that my parents were monsters, and more critically that I was of the same wicked nature as them. He couldn't bear to see me be taken away without doing anything. He intervened and took me back to Barbès to live with him.

My grandfather lost contact with my dad three years before my father eventually died, but he knew deep down that all was not well. His last communication with my father was in Afghanistan. After learning that my father had traveled to the Middle East to join up with Al Qaeda troops, my grandfather dug into his savings and took the first available flight from Paris to Kabul. After a lengthy search which involved paying off multiple radicalized operatives, he found my father and pleaded with him to come home. My grandfather's cries went through one ear and out the other.

I once heard my grandfather tell me that the man he met in Afghanistan was not the boy he raised. That was not the young man he knew as his son; a shift in nature that my grandfather couldn't explain, understand or accept. He was a different human being. He had fire searing in his eyes, frustration in his heart and pain in his soul. His very being was cold. He knew his fate.

My grandfather has been a man of few words for as long as he raised me. He has been very easy on me. He treats me the opposite he did my dad, in hopes that I'll turn out different. He's a good man, but France doesn't see that. The world doesn't see that. I'm not sure they ever will.

As I close the squeaky door behind me, my grandfather replies to me calmly, his voice crusty from decades of smoking cigarettes, "*Wa Alaikum Assalam*, how was your day, Zinedine?"

I always say good. My day was good. I can't bear to lay my problems on my grandfather, he's dealt with too much in his life.

"*Alhamdulillah*, it was good," I reply.

"We have to go into the city today, my old friend Raphaël is sick."

Raphaël is probably the only native French man my grandfather has been close with, ever since my parents died. Before 2004, my grandfather was as well-respected as an Algerian living in Barbès could be. But ever since his son became the most hated man in all of western Europe, he has become public enemy number one. After the tragedies, nearly all his connections cut ties with him immediately. Raphaël, though, stayed by his side and helped him through it all. If it weren't for Raphaël's recommendation and legal assistance, my grandfather would have never been allowed to adopt me in the first place, as he was labeled a threat by the French government. Raphaël has become like a second grandfather to me, so I had no problem visiting him, even if it meant making the arduous, gloomy trip across this tragic city I call home.

It's always a long ride on the metro. Although it is only about ten minutes, it feels like an eternity every time. You know that feeling when you recognize someone, but you're not sure where from? That's what everyone sees in me when they stare me down on the metro. They see my features and they know they recognize me. I always just pray to God they don't remember where they recognize me from. I pray to God that the masses don't see him when they look in my eyes. They don't tend to. They just see an Algerian kid. A thug, a troubled *beur*, probably a thief, maybe a terrorist.

When we got to Raphaël's apartment, it was pretty clear he was on his last legs. This would probably be the last time I'd ever see him. He'd been ill for a while, but I didn't expect him to be taken from us this quickly. He chatted with my grandfather for a while, and out of respect, I didn't eavesdrop. When we were about to leave, I gave Raphaël a hug and thanked him for everything. He softly spoke words that will stick with me forever:

"Zinedine, you are special. You're not just like the other kids raised by the streets. You have the power to raise the streets along with yourself."

He took a sip of his tea and cleared his throat.

"Despite what you may think, despite what the world may think, you aren't just another thug. You aren't destined to just be another thug. You are a product of an incredibly unfortunate yet very unique environment, and this could haunt you, or it could set you free. Now go out there into the world and make your grandfather proud."

My grandfather and I thanked Raphaël one last time. I took one last glance at him before walking out of his apartment. I knew I'd never get to look back again. That's a sensation that can tug at your heartstrings if you let it.

On the ride home, I thought deeply about Raphaël's words. How could I make Raphaël proud? How could I make my grandfather proud? My grandfather always wanted my father to be a footballer. My father tried his best, but nothing came of it. He hung out with the wrong crowd. He was discriminated against, then eventually was radicalized into believing that soccer was a game played only by infidel westerners. I wish I could fulfill that dream for my grandfather, and become the footballer my dad couldn't, but I simply don't have the talent. Even if I worked hard, I'd never catch up to those more talented than me. Sometimes I dream of pulling on the famous blue jersey of France for people who gave me nothing, and repaying them with magic, just like the man who inspired my name. That would surely show them. That would surely make them eat their words. Maybe in an alternate universe that would be possible, but in this one I am stuck with the fate that God wrote for me.

Soon enough, nighttime arrived, as did the all-familiar existential crisis. Not my first and most certainly not my last. Raphaël's words still running through my head, angry thoughts flooded my mind. What options do I even have in this life? Why my parents? Why me!? Why was I dragged into such an unforgiving world, in such an unforgiving context? Why does it even matter!? I was angry. I was livid at existence itself. I wished I never had knowledge of this life. I wished I wasn't here now and it wasn't too late. I cried alone that night, not getting a minute of sleep. My soggy eyes stared blankly towards the broken fan on the ceiling. I didn't dare ever talking to anyone about my problems. Why would I show weakness? In the streets, you have to be tough. If anything gets to you, you can never show it. Even with my best friends I will never show them my vulnerabilities. After hours of tossing, turning and yearning for some relief from my mind, I finally fell asleep.

After nights like that, going to school the next day is always bizarre. You get ready, limbs sore, eyes red, music loud. French-Algerian rap duo PNL's mellow track "Uranus" rang in my ears. The lyrics struck a chord, hitting far too close to home;

> The moon won't always be full
> My heart won't always be empty
> And late at night, I lurk around,
> waiting for my pain to transform into hatred
> Like dad, I want them to fear us

Was I destined to end up like my father? I know I am better than that, but I know part of me feels like that's where my anger would lead me to hell. My dad, as diabolical of a person as he was, was a genius. His intelligence was well-documented by French authorities. My grandfather once told me that nothing ever hurt him more than watching his son's pain and tears transform into rage. With nowhere else to turn, the products of his mind took on a new, destructive form. Our unforgiving world betrayed him, and so he betrayed the world in even more unforgiving circumstances.

Walking through the school hallway, I saw Mamadou. He dapped me up. Mamadou's been a friend of mine for as long as I could remember. He has dark skin and blonde highlights in his hair and can rarely be spotted wearing anything but a Senegalese Sadio Mane jersey. He is one of the most kind-hearted people I have ever met, but he's always on edge, skeptical of others' intentions. He's a tough young man. Over the years, I've seen him getting bruised up from street fights. I know he's a spectacular person, but deep down, in a place he would never show the world, this place has broken him. France doesn't see that. The world doesn't see that. Quite frankly, though, I think he prefers it that way.

"Homie, get the crew. You, me, Wissam and Ibrahim are going out tonight." Mamadou told me.

Sounded like a plan. Maybe I could forget the hell I went through the night before.

"Meet me at Sofiane's place, we'll get something to eat and then play some soccer. Tell the guys."

After school, we all met up at the usual spot. Sofiane's restaurant has a deteriorating sign outside that says "Pizza and Sandwiches," but the actual menu is composed of merguez, couscous and a further assortment of North African food. Just a short walk from school, it was one of the formative pieces of my childhood. Sofiane, the restaurant's owner, was my father's best friend when they were children. Sofiane's father met my grandfather in a restaurant in 1982 in Saint-Denis, where they watched Algeria play in their first ever World Cup. In 1979, Sofiane and my father were born. They grew up together in Barbès. According to my grandfather, they did everything together - back then, all they had was each other. So when my father left for Afghanistan in 2002, it's fair to say Sofiane was heartbroken. Hell, my father never even told him. Even though Sofiane never saw him again, he still keeps their childhood photos up in the restaurant kitchen. Sometimes I see him glance at the pictures, look up to the ceiling, close his eyes, and instinctively continue cooking. Seeing how my father hurt Sofiane - that's been one of the most crushing parts of my father's demise. I guess I could avoid Sofiane altogether, and then I wouldn't have to think about my father. But I don't want to do that. Sofiane has essentially been my father for as long as I can remember. He never had children of his own. He never got married. He could never outrun the demons that had chased him since morning of March 10, 2004, when he turned on the news to see the name "Mohamed Zenoud" plastered next to images of a Kalashnikov, a suicide vest and a flag of Al-Qaeda. I walked into Sofiane's place. None of the crew were there yet. I greeted him as usual.

He quickly looked at my eyes and inquired. "Little bro, you get any sleep last night? You high? Your eyes are so red."

I generally don't say much. This wouldn't be any different.

I just looked at Sofiane and quietly responded. "It was a long night. Lots of homework."

If there was one person I was going to truly open up to, it would be Sofiane, but I can't even let him in. I wish I could. I don't know why I can't. I just can't put what I truly want to say into words. So, yeah, I stay silent.

"Keep doing good in school, kid. You'll be ok, just keep your head up. You want the usual, I assume?" Sofiane said, with a slight chuckle.

"You already know, *shokran amu.*"

Mamadou entered a few minutes after I ordered, on the phone with his uncle. With a very uncomfortable look on his face, he quickly concluded the call before washing it all off and putting on a smile. Mamadou greeted me in a buzzed tone.

"*Salam*, bro," he had his trademark smirk on his face.

Ibrahim and Wissam joined us after a short while. They seemed too tired and too out of it to even have a proper conversation. There was an uneasy and irregular amount of tension in the air. Mamadou seemed nervous. Wissam still seemed bitter, as though he never really got over being released from the Paris Saint Germain Academy. Ibrahim, mentally, was somewhere else entirely. And where was I? I don't know, I couldn't really tell. I felt an unusually anxious feeling. My friends and I - we'd grown up in an era where pain had become so glamorized. Depression, tragedy, suffering, mental health issues, addiction, a life of tears, all glamorized and craved by the masses.

Suddenly, regret is all around you. Suddenly, sadness is happiness, which, at least to me, makes absolutely no sense. I could feel my crew succumbing to the basic desires and characteristics of a society that we had been able to avoid for so long.

Suddenly we were outside, kicking the ball around as we always do, and Wissam was mixing lean to cope with his problems. He didn't feel guilty at all. He didn't wonder what his parents would say, nor did he question his actions. Wissam didn't have to wonder if he was wrong. No, his actions and feelings had been pre-approved - by the music in his earbuds, by the videos on his phone, by his very own role models. Suddenly, Ibrahim was demanding some cough syrup. Suddenly, we had become the teenagers France has always wanted us to be. Suddenly, we were troublemakers, we were drug addicts, we were thieves. Suddenly, we longed for agony.

I asked myself why? It seemed to be some complicated mix of genetic predisposition, historical friction, and our conflicting upbringings. It was tragic, but ironically, that made it all the more intoxicating, infatuating and intriguing.

I was completely aware of my surroundings when I headed home that night. I unlocked the door and saw my grandfather asleep on the couch. I tiptoed to my bed and laid down. I didn't know what to think. I didn't want to think. I turned off the light, put on my headphones, and listened to "100 Rêves" by DTF, letting these words sing me to sleep.

How do you become a man without the example of a father?

I want to make a million before they bury me

I want their jaws to drop, to make them shut up without commentary

Chapter 2: 100 Rêves: July 12, 2017

"*Sbala elkhair.* Zinedine, there is some bread and *msemmen* on the table."

"Thank you, *Djiddah.*"

It has been two months since that night. Ever since then, it has just been more of the same. More nights with the gang, more drugs, more trouble, more crimes, more questions, more insomnia, more pain. That's what we wanted though, isn't it? The wonderful part of having had my childhood is that there has never been external pressure to succeed. Everyone expects my failure, except for me, and even my faith in myself is questionable. Society has always set low expectations for me. My education, upbringing and the entirety of my existence are essentially just damage control. As Raphaël told me, it could haunt me or it could set me free. I understood that, and I felt myself caught in between those two distinct and separate futures.

"What are your plans today, Zinedine?" my grandfather said to me, as I downed the bread and *msemmen* that were on the table.

"I'm going to kick the ball around with Ibrahim inch-Allah, only if you are ok with that, of course," I replied.

"That's fine, just stay out of trouble," he responded.

I met Ibrahim near Sofiane's. I could see the extraordinary amount of gel in his jet black hair from across the street. We started walking towards the sports complex.

"How've you been, bro?" Ibrahim asked.

"I have been alright, *hamdulillah*, same old same old," I replied.

It felt as cold as ever. Ibrahim felt so preoccupied with something. He was searching for something and he didn't have any clue what it was. He was trying to understand a world outside of the 18th arrondissement of Paris, a world outside this city, a world he had never experienced. A world he was desperate to comprehend. We continued to the field in silence. For the first time ever, it felt like there was nothing to discuss.

"Do you know why Paris Saint Germain released Wissam last year? He opens up to you more than me, and he never goes into detail about what happened."

Ibrahim slowly turned to me and gave me a response I would have never expected from him, "Bro, if he hasn't told you, there's a reason."

I felt like an outsider. I didn't have the heart to reply. I was insulted, but as I usually do, I pinned the blame on myself. I probably did something wrong. When you grow up like I did, that's just how you think. You are always the monster.

Just before we got to the complex, a man with light skin, light eyes and light hair locked eyes with me. I felt a peculiar energy radiating from him. As we exchanged stares, he looked at me with pure hatred. Suddenly, without a word, the man sprinted towards me and shoved me to the ground. I immediately got up and put a fist to his jaw. I was already covered in scrapes and blood from the initial confrontation, but my adrenaline, ego and fury masked the pain. He must've been over 6 feet tall and could've easily overpowered me. That thought didn't even cross my mind. In the moment, all I could think was that this man must've been racist, mentally ill, or both.

But then, as we stood up, the man spoke in a disgusted voice, "He killed my son. I could kill his."

That's when it hit me. That's when the list of victims flashed through my mind. That's when I saw this man's son in his eyes, just as he saw my father in mine.

Before I could start to explain anything to this man (as if there was anything to explain), the police were already arriving at the scene. I was already in handcuffs, a cop slapping me across my already rough, scraped face. Ibrahim simply watched in awe, still holding the soccer ball as they hauled me away, as they put me, a 16-year-old boy who had been assaulted, in the backseat of the cop car, as I was led to a new, harrowing chapter in my life.

I didn't know where the police were going to take me. There are street fights all the time in Barbés. I didn't even instigate the brawl. I was seething.

I looked at the officer before he started the engine and said with a raised voice, "Aye, officer, where are you taking me? What did I do? Look at my bruises! I am 16! That man should be going to jail!"

It only took 3 words for the officer to break me.

"Shut up, terrorist."

I wanted to open the door and throw him out. I wanted him to feel my wrath. I was about to scream expletives and curse out the injustice. But then, I remembered my grandfather telling me to stay out of trouble, the sound of his voice ringing through my ears. I stopped myself. It took all the will and self-control I had. I sat there with a slumped posture and watery eyes, knowing that the car was headed towards my home.

I stood outside as the officers approached the front door. My heart was beating faster than my mind could even process. The cuffs were so tight that they felt like they were going to rip my hands off.

My grandfather opened the door, and immediately whispered, "*Astaghfirullah, astaghfirullah, astaghfirullah,*" under his charcoal breath.

A somber repentance, bracing for the second worst interaction with law enforcement in his life. One of the two police officers stepped forward and informed my grandfather of the supposed situation.

"Mr. Zenoud, your grandson assaulted the father of a victim from the attacks in 2004. Due to his familial ties and the court order, we must take him into our custody today."

I immediately countered, "I didn't do it, I promise. I did nothing! I was attacked! *WAllah!*"

The officers quickly silenced me. I expected my grandfather to finally erupt and express fury at me for all the times he has remained patient throughout my childhood and adolescence, but instead, he just looked at me. He stared into me with his weary, soulful, brown eyes. It felt like he was seeing inside me. He let out a colossal sigh.

"I know, Zinedine. I know." He replied to me.

His words were simply a translation of what his eyes had communicated to me seconds before. Without any sign of sympathy, the lifeless officers continued on with what felt like a manifesto.

"We will update you on the situation regarding Zinedine, however considering his paternal link to the primary assailant of the 2004 attacks and the release term you both signed when he was allowed to remain with you, he will be required to serve twelve months in prison, despite his age. According to Zinedine's records, he scored extraordinarily on standardized tests, in both the academic and social areas. We can conclude from this data that he was aware of the action he was taking. This, under French law, is fair grounds for this deferred prosecution."

My grandfather nodded his head in compliance, and the officer gave him a judgmental, smug glare. I walked back to the car, completely out of tune with reality. My mind wasn't present. I looked bitterly towards the bright blue sky. I was searching for something, and I had no clue what it was. I was trying to understand a world outside of the 18th arrondissement of Paris. A world outside this city. A world I have never experienced. A world I was desperate to comprehend.

The drive to the prison took around 45 minutes, but it felt much, much shorter than that. I still wasn't sure where they would take me. I thought that maybe it would be a youth correctional center or a local jail. When I got to the infamous Fleury-Mérogis Prison, I couldn't really believe what was happening. Me, I was going to the most dangerous prison in all of France, and the largest prison in all of Europe. This morning, I left my home to play soccer, never expecting that by the afternoon I'd be entering a literal hell on earth. And all because of my name. So much for *Liberté, Equalité, Fraternité.*

I could have been full of rage, or upset, or depressed. The truth is, I was all of those things. I was just in too much shock to come to terms with it. I got out of the car, my wrists still paralyzed by steel. The officers took all the belongings that I had on me, and led me to a small, cramped room. It was scorching inside, and I could feel the heaviness and strife in the air.

"Change into your uniform so we can lead you to your cell. As you are so closely linked to 2004, we don't even have to go through the hassle of a trial. We take terrorism very seriously here in France, isn't that right?"

I could hear the mockery in the officer's voice. I kept myself from replying, because if I did, it wouldn't have been with words.

I got changed into the white prison garment. I never thought I would be putting in on, but now that I was, I wasn't surprised that it had come to this. I felt nauseous when the uniform rubbed against my skin. The guard rushed me to my cell.

On my way, I scanned the prison. It didn't look so horrendous from the outside, but once you were in, it was sickening. The living conditions were inhumane. Most of the guards abused their power. Seventy percent of the prison population was Muslim, and radicalization was happening at every corner. It was like I could see back in time, walk down the same stray path as my father did. It made my stomach rumble. Once I got to my cell, the walls were stained with dried blood. The room was microscopic. I couldn't wait for the guard to just leave.

"There you go, Inmate #1618. Now you're with your own kind - alongside *Djamel* and *Salah*." He chuckled as he left me inside the unfiltered fish tank, I would be calling my home for the next year.

As the door to my cell slammed closed, the door separating the reality of my life from my ability to process that timeline of events busted open. I knew the recent history of the Fleury-Mérogis Prison. The list of inmates went on and on. Amedy Coulibaly, a young French-Senegalese man, and Chérif and Saïd Kouachi, two French-Algerian brothers. Together, they committed the coordinated attacks across Paris in 2015, including the infamous Charlie Hebdo shooting. The man who mentored all three of them, Djamel Beghal, was also an inmate. Salah Abdeslam, a Belgian-Moroccan and the last of the seven terrorists responsible for the horrific attacks in Paris in November 2015 still alive was kept within these walls. Jacques Mesrine, a French mobster who is one of the most iconic criminals France has ever seen broke out of this prison.

Although I didn't have any music, the lyrics of PNL's "Porte de Mesrine," a track about none other than Jacques Mesrine himself, ran through my mind.

> We'll soon be ok, or else we'll perish
> The world deserves it
> Homie, we can't change who we are
> I live a life that I'll never have

Tarik Andrieu, the older brother of the duo, had also seen time in this prison for extensive drug trafficking charges.

Chapter 3: Désolé: February 2018

It has been 6 months since I was taken into custody. These have been the longest and most agonizing months of my life. I feel trapped by the system. I've been left with my own thoughts, and nothing to distract me from my nihilistic nature other than the pain, agony, and hatred in the eyes of my fellow inmates. An inmate. That is what I am now. If you pulled up a summary of my life and showed it to an average citizen of the world, what would they say? What could they say? All of my lineage has led up to this very moment. All of it ultimately led up to this moment in which their latest descendant lies in this rusty, rickety, rotten prison in the south of Paris. They could have never imagined what it would have led to, but regardless, time and fate continue to go on and surprise us all. Time will drag you through existence, because whether you are conscious of it or not, time will continue.

That's what I think about during lonely nights in my cell. There are no diversions. I sleep on an infected, intoxicated mattress above a terrorist. I am not as fazed as I should be. This is what the world has always told me I deserved, only now their expectations have become my reality.

The first few weeks here were the most difficult. I'd glance around the establishment, watching psychotic men tune into heartbreaking news stations from faraway lands. Multiple prisoners tried to lure me into the trap of radical Islam, and the most grievous part was that I had to actively try to ignore an emotion that was stirring inside; an emotion which urged me to consider what these deeply flawed individuals had to say. I felt my demons relishing the thought of a purpose. My heart sunk in my stomach as these men with crooked teeth and crooked minds attempted to indoctrinate me.

"Why are you here Zinedine? Why are we here? Because of this infidel country! That is why!"

"Follow your father! It is in your blood mashAllah, you are meant to be a soldier of the caliphate like those before you!"

One of the men who tried to radicalize me was my cellmate, 24-year-old Houari Abdelkader. He was born in Corbeil-Essonnes to an Algerian father and Moroccan mother. For the first few weeks, he didn't tell me anything more than that. However, as we have gotten more comfortable, he has revealed more and more about his life and how he ended up in this place. Houari's childhood and adolescence were eerily similar to so many North Africans in France. He grew up idolizing soccer players and rappers, he dropped out of school, he got involved in the gangs, and was sentenced far too heavily for the crimes he committed. He will be in prison until he is twenty-seven. During his time here, he has transformed from a petty criminal into a terrorist. He plans on travelling to Iraq as soon as he gets out. I can tell that he's clearly in need of psychological treatment, but it's not like France has any system in place to help mentally ill social outcasts. France doesn't want to accommodate people like Houari, it wants to lock them away.

Sometimes, late at night in our cell, he shows a glimpse of his former self to me. Sometimes we talk about rap or even soccer.

He quickly reverts back to the hard, heartless persona he attempts to put on. Even though it's just a facade, I know that as time goes on, it would soon become second nature.

The prison guards don't help matters. I stay out of their way. The looks in their eyes are arguably more nefarious than the eyes of the terrorists. They blame us. They blame Islam. They blame our "barbaric" African intuition. They blame everything other than the evident social and historical injustice that clearly exists in France. Toxicity and conflict fill the air and the only way to avoid them is to stay neutral and quiet. That is how I will get out of here. Prison has taught me patience.

My grandfather comes and visits me every time he gets the chance. I never really have much to say. Prison is exactly what Barbès had always made out to be. In our last few meetings, we talked about my future, what happens when I finally get out. I have five months left. I know my education is basically over. We have no clue what the future could possibly hold, but like I said, time will go on regardless of whether we are ready for it to or not. I don't even care. I don't have the courage to care about where life leads me. I could die right now. That wouldn't change the world. Even if it did, what's the significance in that? What is the significance in anything within comprehension? I don't want anything that I can understand. I don't want to go to heaven. I don't want to go to hell. I don't want to live forever. I don't want to die. There is nothing that can fulfill me except creating an illusion strong enough that my senses and consciousness are distracted from whatever keeps plaguing my soul. In prison, there is no such thing. There is only time. Time that continues to move at a startling rate. Faster. Then slower. Never matching your expectations. You can try to predict the future, but it's so rarely correct. Things never turn out how you think they were meant to turn out, they just turn out how they were meant to be. Fate is fate. It cannot be altered.

Chapter 4: Loin Des Etoiles: July 14, 2018

Many of the prisoners were livid when they heard the news. Many were absolutely exuberant. It was only the second time in history and the first time in twenty years: France was in the 2018 World Cup Final.

The match would take place on July 15th. My release date is July 14th. Back in February, I'd already noticed that I would get out just in time to watch the World Cup final, but now that I knew it would be France competing in the event, I was more ecstatic than I can ever remember being. Words couldn't describe my excitement - I was just waiting for the moment my grandfather would pick me up. We'd go home and watch the historic match together. It gave me something to look forward to while stuck in an environment in which it was so hard to smile about anything. As I was straightening up my cell, I was thrilled to know I'd never have to see that chamber again. I didn't think I could ever return. That room knew more about me than I know about myself. Houari glimpsed at me. He opened his dry mouth.

"Let's hope this country loses tomorrow inch-Allah, yeah? Call me when you get out bro, you know what you want."

I thought I didn't care what would happen to me or anyone else. Intellectually, I guess I didn't. I knew better than to care. When I replied to Houari, it was purely instinctual. There wasn't any thought that went into it. I looked right into his confused, brown eyes. His greasy, brown bangs were obstructing his vision.

"You know who had the same name as you Houari? Houari Boumediene. The greatest Algerian president of all time. Houari Boumediene famously had a very neutral stance when it came to foreign policy. Boumediene was a strict Muslim. I'd bet anything your father named you after this man. Go read about it. Call me when you get out bro. You don't know what you want right now. You've been brainwashed. My father was just like you and, trust me, you don't want to go down that path. It ruined his life, it ruined mine. It's the only reason I even know you. Good luck my brother. I wish for you to be brought back to the straight path."

I was just waiting for Houari to interrupt me. I thought for sure he was going to shut me out or come strike my skin. But he didn't. He just gazed over wearily. He could have been dead for all I knew. He was looking in my general direction, but not at me, or even at the maroon and graphite grey wall behind me. His attention didn't seem tuned into anything at all. It felt like he was in another universe, in another time. He wasn't on my wavelength. I simply could not perceive his soul in that moment - and therefore could not fully understand how it made me feel. For the first time in my life, I was in a situation which struck me as inexplicably unnatural. I felt like that moment in time wasn't meant to happen. Without a sound, Houari turned to lay the other way on his bed. I couldn't read him. I didn't know how he had taken my words.

What he said to me gave me an interesting perspective on things. He said to me that I knew what I wanted, in a tone suggesting he had no doubt in his mind that his purpose in life was to wage war. It's an intriguing, yet incredibly disheartening mental collapse that leads human beings to conclusions such as these. Houari wasn't born this way. He wasn't even necessarily brought up this way. He was lost, and organized violence gave him a purpose - something France was unable to offer. For people like Houari, happy endings are an illusion. If you wait for the satisfaction of watching the world fix itself in accordance with your values, then you'll live a life of sorrow. Life's not fair, and it was never meant to be fair. Life is far too complex to ever be considered fair.

As I headed to the reception to meet my grandfather my body began to ache. My vision got blurry. None of it seemed real. It was almost like the fact that I was in prison is only beginning to actually hit me now that I was leaving it. My head was swirling like a tornado as I filled out the seemingly endless paperwork given to me on my way out. I couldn't wait to see the summer sky. I couldn't wait to be back on the other side.

"You enjoy your vacation?" My grandfather smiled and playfully punched my arm on our way out.

For the first time in what felt like forever, I laughed. I truly laughed. I looked over at my grandfather in his blue beret, linen pants and leather shoes. Where would I be without him? It doesn't matter where I would be, but regardless, the insignificant thought of where I could have ended up still makes me shiver. I owe everything to him.

The ride home whizzed by. I didn't expect my grandfather to bring up anything serious or talk about prison at all. I was right, he didn't. He just wanted to talk about the World Cup final.

"So who's winning, Zizou?"

Honestly, I wasn't sure who was going to take the trophy. Croatia had done well to get to their first ever World Cup final, and with players like Luka Modric and Ivan Rakitic, they definitely had a chance. However, they were also massive underdogs. The French team was absolutely loaded in every single position. Paul Pogba, N'golo Kante, Raphael Varane, Antoine Griezmann and of course - 19-year-old Kylian Mbappe.

"I think France will win. The French team is just too talented to lose this final."

My grandfather gave me an innocent laugh and continued to be overwhelmingly kind and upbeat.

"Zinedine, if you want to invite your friends over to watch the final, you can. I am sure you would like to see them."

I loved my friends, but maybe this was a moment for just my grandfather and me. I wasn't ready to be interrogated by my friends about the last twelve months just yet.

"*Shokran,* but it's okay. I think we should just watch the final on our own."

We finally pulled into the driveway. I walked up to the front door, and opened it, hearing its familiar creak. Nostalgia flooded through me. I had finally returned. Who knew that this place, which I once took for granted, would be so elating to come back to? Perspective really is everything.

The whole world had their eyes glued to Moscow's Luzhniki Stadium as the referee blew his whistle to commence the 2018 World Cup Final.

The first fifteen minutes were nerve-racking to say the least. Good ball movement from the Croatians, with the French front line barely able to touch the ball. You could feel the tension through the TV screen. It was as if the players' hearts were racing faster than their legs were.

In the 17th minute, Marcelo Brozovic clipped down Antoine Griezmann in a dangerous position outside the box. Griezmann himself would be the one to step up for the delivery, and as he whipped it into the mixer, Croatian forward Mario Mandzukic redirected the ball into his own net. France was 1-0 up in very scrappy circumstances.

"Very unlucky," said my grandfather.

Despite the French goal, Croatia continued to dominate the match. In the 28th minute, Ivan Perisic rewarded them with a spectacular left footed volley to the right side of the goal. Although we were hoping for a French victory, a goal like this in a World Cup final did send some shockwaves through the living room. I was up on my feet as soon as he struck the ball.
"What a strike! They deserve that goal for sure." I uttered.

My grandfather continued where I left off, "*Bah bah bah bah,* you see what a lefty can do?"

I didn't have the heart to tell my grandfather that Perisic was ambidextrous. The match continued with the same incredible intensity that was on display in the first half hour. This was quite the World Cup final.

In the 35th minute, Antoine Griezmann hit an in swinging corner into the Croatian box, and Ivan Perisic went from hero to villain as the ball struck his hand. France were awarded a penalty. Griezmann would be the one to step up and take the responsibility.

"Can you imagine the pressure he must be under? The whole world watching?" my grandfather noted.

Despite that, Griezmann stepped up and calmly converted the penalty. France were back in the lead. The first half ended with France leading 2-1 over Croatia, despite being far from their best. Going into the second period, both sides would have a lot to play for going into the second period. This would be a true test of their character.

"Croatia is playing pretty well. They've just gotten unlucky on two set pieces. You still think France will win this game?" My grandfather chuckled, amused by his doubt.

He always loved trying to push my buttons by going against me. It never works, I always just laugh.

I smiled and responded. "Mbappe will come alive in the second half."

Over the last two years, Parisian-born forward Kylian Mbappe had lit up the football world football one goal at a time. Now nineteen years old, Mbappe broke into the AS Monaco first team at the youthful age of seventeen, scoring goals in the UEFA Champions League against heavyweight teams such as Manchester City and winning Ligue 1 over heavy favorites Paris Saint-Germain. Unlike other wonderkids, Mbappe was not nurtured in a professional academy from a young age, but had to leave Paris and head to Monte Carlo in his teenage years in pursuit of a professional career. Mbappe returned to Paris last summer, being sold to an entity that was once considered the enemy, Paris Saint-Germain. After an incredible debut season with his hometown club, the young superstar was now playing in a World Cup final for his country. He had already made his mark on the tournament, scoring twice versus Argentina in their round of 16 clash. Electrifying pace, illusionistic ball skills, lethal finishing ability; Mbappe had it all, and I was certain he'd be able to use it against the ever-tiring Croatian defense.

Early on in the second half, it had already become clear that the French intended to intimidate the Croatians. After all, they had left Mbappe high up the pitch, so that if any Croatian were to advance towards the French goal, they were forced to remain cautious of the young man's incredible speed. As the Croatians became more anxious to recover a goal, the youthful French side would rely on their dazzling defensive unit to break down any attempt. Once the ball was recovered, they would quickly release Mbappe, who was destined to be effective sooner rather than later.

Just over ten minutes into the second period, Kylian Mbappe scuffed a cross across the box, which landed at the green and silver boots of Antoine Griezmann. The silky center forward, who had been rejected from multiple French clubs in his youth, laid the ball off to Paul Pogba. The Manchester United superstar blasted a shot with his rocket right foot directly into defender Domagoj Vida. The Adidas Telstar Match ball fell right back to the former Juventus midfielder's weaker left foot, and he wouldn't miss the second time. Pogba lasered the ball into the top corner, leaving goalkeeper Danijel Subasic no option but to stop and stare as the ball flew past his grasp into the white webbing behind him. France were well on their way to recapturing the elusive World Cup trophy.

"This is it *Djiddah*, France is winning another World Cup" I stated.

I looked over at my grandfather. He let out a chuckle, and a slight smirk to go along with it. He sipped his mint tea like it was the medication keeping him alive. He swirled the serum around in his cup. I glanced as he gazed at his reflection in the beaming blue tea glass almost every single time he sampled the tea, before carefully setting down the soothing beverage onto the table next to him.

France kept on plugging away, letting their adrenaline carry them closer and closer to euphoria. Just over an hour into the match, French full-back Lucas Hernandez acquired the ball on the left side of the field. Hernandez swiftly squared the ball towards the center of the pitch. Kylian Mbappe latched onto the end of the pass, and quickly cannoned a shot into the bottom left corner of the Croatian net. The teenager wheeled away in celebration as the whole world witnessed what they had all been waiting for. The great Pele was the first teenager to ever score in a World Cup Final. Kylian Mbappe was the second. The boy from Bondy was on top of the world.

Mbappe had the number 10 plastered to the back of his sweaty blue kit, just as Zinedine Zidane had 20 years before, when he led France to victory in the 1998 World Cup Final.

"Your father was nineteen in '98" my grandfather quietly said.

I didn't know whether I was supposed to reply or not. I stayed silent, and my grandfather continued.

"He wasn't too different from the way you are now, Zizou. Less than 6 years after that day, he would be dead. So would hundreds of others. July 12, 1998. That was the last day your father was truly transparent. To me, I never saw my son again after that day."

Staring at the staticky reflection from our television screen in my grandfather's gargantuan eyes was like peeking back in time. We are so closely connected to the past. There is no substantial evidence of the past other than the present. Time quickly forgets what happened yesterday, or what happened twenty years ago. Despite this, it comes to define our present. Applying the same logic, it can be concluded that our future is entirely defined by our present from my perspective in this so-called human condition, that haunts me in every possible way it can. However, when spoken in any language other than those in which my instinctual desire to succeed understands, I know that it does not really matter at all.

There wasn't anything to say in response to my grandfather. His eyes were addicted to the display, clearly contemplating his past - something I was certain he would not express to me. I knew it was time to get up and leave my grandfather with his thoughts. I dragged myself off the couch and began to traipse to the other room. As I exited the premises, my grandfather spoke.

"We have to find you a future, Zizou."

He didn't look me in the eyes as he said it. He was still watching the game. Mario Mandzukic scored a Croatian consolation goal, bringing the score to 4-2. Although his focus was on the game, I still nodded my head in agreement, as though he was analyzing my every move. We both wanted the same thing - but we were not optimistic individuals. When we look at roses, we see it all. We can see the gorgeous flowers. However, the only aspect of it that we can truly comprehend is the jagged thorns hidden below the beauty of the bouquet. When we watch this France team win the World Cup final, we also see it all. We can see the glistening, gleaming World Cup trophy. But perhaps, in even better clarity, we see the grey ghetto most of the squad members came from, before they ever knew a glamorous life at the top. We can't understand a lavish existence. Our senses have never known luxury. A life like ours makes it easier to see the worst in things.

I launched myself onto my bed. I picked up my faulty earbuds and plugged them into my phone. For the first time in a while, I let music distract me from my desolate thoughts. Tonight, my shuffle button matched me with MMZ's "Loin des Étoiles".

> I open my shutters towards the sky,
> I raise my head
> My *Sheitan* (Devil) on the left would like to make me dishonest
> I know, I've got millions of enemies,
> Yeah I've got millions of problems
> But no, I'm not a bad person deep down...
> It's only once things are done
> That I question myself
> I've got qualities and I've got flaws
> Life is tragic, the sky is beautiful

I stared at my broken ceiling fan, the track blasting into my left ear. In my right ear, I was hearing the muffled celebrations of the French team, surely lifting the World Cup trophy Over that, I could hear the tears of my grandfather. And then, very faintly, somewhere among all the noise, I could hear the laughter of my father from the 90's.

> I don't want to see anymore tears
> I don't want to do anymore wrong
> But after all, I'm from the projects...
> Meanwhile, the police commissioner is observing you
> I know these men, this life
> This money, the world, the night
> The evil envies me

I felt tears pooling, hatred pouring out of my soul. The hook of the track came just in time to soothe me.

> Tired of being downstairs
> Far from the stars
> It time to set sail

Already, this moment was stained into the scrapbook of my adolescence. As the melancholy vocals faded away, I made a decision. I couldn't stand to see my grandfather die unfulfilled. I couldn't stand to see this life pass me by. I couldn't stand to see fate reject me. I didn't know how, but I was going to find a way. I was going to become a professional footballer.

Chapter 5: Tel Père Tel Fils: July 15, 2018

As I woke up the next morning, I heard a hush of murmuring emanating from the kitchen. I arose and got dressed, curious to see who my grandfather was hosting this morning. Huh, the first morning I was waking up in my own bed. At least, the first morning since I'd gotten back. I didn't even notice it at first, my mind was too distracted. Still, as I exited my bedroom and entered the kitchen, I contemplated it for a moment.

The second that I entered the kitchen, I was bombarded with hugs. The first to embrace me was Ibrahim. I opened my eyes and smiled as he wrapped himself around me. I could see Wissam, Mamadou and Sofiane all patiently waiting their turn. It was a wonderful moment.

Once the pleasantries were out of the way, we all took a seat around the oak kitchen table. The kitchen was closed off and a tight fit with all of us in it, but it wasn't cramped. It was cozy. It was comfortable. I looked around me at the apartment I grew up in. It wasn't much, but it was a home. If someday I had a wildly successful future, I would still return here despite my illustrious achievements. The wool white walls exuded nostalgia. This very moment was feeding off the fuel of such a sentiment.

"Thank you all for coming to visit me. I missed you all."

Sofiane was the first to respond, "Anything for my little bro. We're all we have. We have to stick together."

He was smiling as he said those words, but as soon as he turned his head and saw me smiling back, it gradually faded and turned into a solemn, gloomy expression.

"Zizou, go hang out with your friends and you can go get something to eat at Sofiane's later," my grandfather stated.

We headed out the creaky door, just like old times. It had been so long. The vibe was unlike it was before I went to jail. It was fresh and rejuvenated. It took Mamadou about 30 seconds before he chuckled out a trademark joke.

"So, Zinedine, how was the prison food? They cook as well as your grandfather?"

Everyone laughed. My grandfather is a stupendous chef.

"Homie, I didn't even bother to eat in prison!"

The mood was electrifying. We forgot where we were, who we were, and how we got there. None of that mattered. The defective soccer ball we were kicking around rolled like a flat tire as we dribbled it on the uneven concrete. Wissam laid off the ball for me, and I showed off some flashy ball skills before flicking the ball off to Ibrahim. Wissam took notice that something was different.

"*Igo*, you play a lot in the prison courtyard Zizou? Your control is a lot better than it was last time I saw you."

I replied, making my intentions clear, "I decided I'm gonna do anything I can to become a professional soccer player."

Wissam gave me a response that I didn't know I needed, "You know I will support you in anything you do. I will support you in this journey. But the footballing world is unforgiving Zizou. You just got out of jail. You are 17 and you have never been in an academy. I will give you all the support I have to give, because this crew is all I have. Just know it will be hard. It won't just be hard. It will be near impossible- but hey, what do you have to lose?"

It was a reality check. Wissam was in the academy of one of the world's biggest clubs, Paris Saint Germain, for more than 7 years. He knew what he was saying.

The crew seemed to nod in agreement. I was ready to give everything, but I was ready for failure at the same time.

We continued to pass the ball around and catch up. The air was unusually fresh and crisp. The streets were filled with French citizens proudly wearing the deep sea blue or pastel white football jerseys of their nation. The entire country was intoxicated by a footballing fever I had never seen before. In France, North Africa, and throughout the world, really, soccer cannot truly be described as a sport. Soccer is a lifestyle. It influences the decisions of the masses all across the globe. Soccer directly contributed to the independence movement of Algeria in the 50's and early 60's. Alongside Algeria's massacres, political corruption, war heroes, and inhumane conflicts, football was always a constant. In the 50 years since its independence was gained from France in 1962, Algeria has still had football. In almost all ways imaginable, whether it is culturally, religiously, linguistically or politically, Algeria has had a tangled history with France. Soccer is no exception to this. When Algeria played Belgium in the 2014 World Cup, 9 of the 11 players that started for the Desert Foxes were born and raised in the nation of their former colonizers. When France won the World Cup yesterday, Nabil Fekir got his hands on the trophy. Nabil Fekir has two Algerian parents. Kylian Mbappe became a global phenomenon. Kylian Mbappe's mother was a professional Algerian handball player. No matter how much of France would love to bolt away from their gruesome history with Africa, and more specifically Algeria, they can't. They never can. We won't ever let them.

We started in the direction of Sofiane's. I couldn't wait to open the door and smell the cuisine. Sofiane cooks well, but it has never been about the food. It's the ambiance. The ambiance of Sofiane's fuels whatever in my mind can recognize and put into words the struggle of my upbringing. Without a staple location like that, I don't think I would have a reference which I could use to convey how I feel about my existence.

I took a second and looked around at the *miff*. Ibrahim was dressed in baby blue Adidas pants with glossy white stripes and an Amine Harit Schalke jersey with similar base colors. Mamadou sported an ashy black parka and some Nike joggers. Wissam had a PSG jacket, black Adidas pants, and some classic Adidas sambas to top it off. I was rocking a pitch black velvet PUMA jogging suit that Sofiane had gotten me as a gift a couple years prior. It was starting to get too small, but I didn't care. It has too much swazz for me to stop wearing it.

We entered Sofiane's, and he started laughing immediately after he saw us, "*Salam*, you're still wearing the suit little bro? You've spent a year in prison and you still don't think it's too small?"

"It's too sick to put it down!" I replied ecstatically.

"I'll get you a new one little bro, don't worry."

Of all the flaws that North Africans can have, generosity does not tend to be one. Sure, you cannot generalize an entire race, but North Africans are consistently munificent. I haven't been to Algeria since I was very young, but my grandfather always says that there is an unexplainable connection between the citizens. Sofiane doesn't have much money at all, but he would buy me a new velvet PUMA jogging suit without hesitation. Maybe he wouldn't have enough money to get some of the clothes he wants, or the dinner he is craving, but he would do it. I won't let him, but he would. No questions asked.

It didn't take long before Sofiane brought out my usual dish; a *merguez* sandwich with fries and mayonnaise between the bread and lamb sausage. As we were wolfing down the platters, Ibrahim made a valid point.

"So, I hate to be the pessimist, but what club is going to take someone who literally just got out of prison? No matter how good you are?"

He was right. I have a criminal record, and I had no idea how to overcome that in the world of football. It would already be hard enough working my way up the leagues considering the fact that I have never been in an academy. With a criminal record attached to that, my chances were astronomically low.

Sofiane overheard our conversation, "What, Zizou, you tryna go pro?" He declared from the kitchen.

Sofiane marched out into the main area of his restaurant. He sat down on the bright red, padded seat right next to us. He took off his stained apron and took a deep breath.

"Little bro, we know you are a great kid. The French coaches picking you? All they see is the last name "Zenoud" and a criminal record. You have the ability, and you work hard. Unfortunately, considering your circumstances, that just isn't enough."

Every vein in my body boiled, only because I knew he was right. My soul was stolen from me by the past.

"What if I went to Algeria?" I replied out of desperation. I knew it was a farfetched thought.

My friends had grim looks on their faces as they saw me fall victim to the unjust nature of the world we live in.

"You really think the French government is going to let you travel to Algeria right after you get out of prison? That's not even considering all the other factors as to why making it in Algeria is near impossible."

I was empty inside. Pursuing my dream of playing professional soccer was always going to be virtually unachievable. What it does is pass time. It saved me from the agony of stalling and impatiently waiting for something more. The present wasn't just solemn - it was torturously menacing.

"You know guys, I'm gonna head home. I'm really tired. Thank you all for the support and it was amazing to see you all again. We will see what the future holds *inshAllah.*"

I shook them all up and started on my way home. The truth was that I was wide awake. I just needed some time alone. I was feeling myself begin to get too emotional and schmaltzy to ever be around the crew. I could feel the velour material of my tracksuit swiping at my skin. It felt no different than the prison garment. The scorching July sun blinded me from looking up. All I could see was either at my level or under me. My fists were ferociously clenched, holding the vast amount of anger that was developing throughout me. Just as I was approaching the apartment, I felt my phone buzz. My vision was fuzzy because of the immense water that I was holding in my eyes. I was doing everything I could to make sure that they didn't fall out and stream down my aloof face. I looked down and could just make out the name. It was Sofiane. I picked it up.

"Salam Sofiane, what's up"? I said right away.

Sofiane replied with excitement. "So after you left the restaurant, I decided to call up my brother Zakaria. You met him a long time ago when you were much younger. In 2014, he moved to the United States. He works as a chef at a restaurant just outside of Seattle, and he told me that his coworker owns a 4th division American team in the area called OSA FC. I asked him if you would be able to head over and trial, and he said that you can go and stay with him. You can ask your grandfather if you want, and I can talk to him as well of course. Let me know soon inch-Allah if you are interested little bro."

I couldn't help but begin to smile as I heard him say the words. The tears began to fall out of my eyes, but it wasn't glum. It was a resurgence and a sense of hope. I sprinted home and opened the door to talk to my grandfather about the possibility. As soon as I entered the door and greeted him, I proposed the idea.

"So I just talked to Sofiane on the phone about five minutes ago. He told me that his brother Zakaria who lives in the United States knows someone who owns a 4th division soccer club. He told me that I can stay with his brother and tryout for the club. Do you think I can go sometime grandfather? My opportunities are miniscule in France."

My grandfather replied with wrath that I hadn't seen from him in a long time. "Zizou, you think it's that easy? To get you into the United States? To go and make the team? To pay for a plane ticket? It's not! You can't be so naive!"

He was shaking intensely, and his wide eyes tore through my flesh as he said it. I curled back up into my shell.

"Okay, I understand." I replied quietly to my grandfather.

I walked over to my room and leaped face first onto my bed. I laid there in an idle position for the rest of the day. I felt less and less rage and more and more sorrow as time ticked on.

I only left the room a single time in the next 24 hours which was to eat dinner with my grandfather that night. I could not eat much, even though the *couscous* was sublime. I immediately returned to my room to close my eyes and see nothing. No dreams. No nightmares. It was just dark. That was more soul-stirring than words can describe.

I don't know how much I slept that night. It's all just a blur in my mind. The vibe was atmospheric. It felt like the world was chasing my very being out of the realms of reality. I was vexed at my perspective, which seemed like a habitual part of my life at this point. The next morning at the crack of dawn, I heard my grandfather open the unlocked door of my room. The sky still spilled a gloomy navy shade as the sun started to rise.

"*Saba El Kheir* Zizou, how are you?"

I urged myself to get up and replied. "*Hamdulillah*, how about you *Djiddah*?"

What he said next flipped my world upside down.

Chapter 6: American Dream: July 16, 2018

I swiftly sat up on the bare mattress that laid in the middle of my bland and somber room. As per usual, my grandfather was already dressed up for the day despite the fact that it was still dark outside. He proceeded to speak words of astronomical proportions - stating it all in a calm tone that only he is capable of.

"Last night I spoke on the phone with one of Raphael's old friends in the government. I asked him about the possibility of getting you over to the United States."

He took a slight pause and cleared his throat. My heart was participating in a marathon. I could feel my nerves jangling like loose keys. It is madness how much our perspective defines our happiness.

"He told me that he can get you on a flight to Seattle today and today only. I linked him with Sofiane's brother and they are gonna get you some papers so that you'll be able to legally live and work there. Your flight is tonight at 7. Get your things ready by then, I won't wait for you if you are late. We have to be ready to head to the airport by 2:30."

My heart, which had previously been beating so fast, stopped. The whole world stopped. Time stopped. Everything within comprehension halted itself. I jumped out of the bed and threw my arms around my grandfather.

"Thank you, thank you, thank you" I said with an uncharacteristically squeaky and shaky voice. I couldn't stop saying thank you. I couldn't ever repay him.

He made his way to the rusty door and stopped in his tracks as he opened it. "Zizou, this is your chance. In life. This is what we've always waited for. Make the most of it inch'Allah."

I immediately began throwing my belongings into the colossus suitcase that had been collecting dust in the closet for years. As I pulled it out, I had to tear off the tags that had been attached almost twenty years previously, when my grandfather rushed to the Middle East to attempt to save my father. Now, I fly to the United States to try to save myself.

The velvet Puma jogging suit was the last thing I could stuff in the suitcase before fastening it closed. I had finished tidying up my room and packing by noon, which was much earlier than I had expected to. I decided to go swing by Sofiane's one last time. I didn't know when I would get to be back home. Barbés is home, whether I like it or not.

I walked through the ever rampant streets of the banlieues of Paris. These roads are alive. As I contemplated the significance of the concrete that I traversed, PNL did the same in my headphones on their aggressive track "Dans ta rue".

I'm in your town, I'm in your streets,
It's grim, I'm smiling upside down

The echo of the track faded as I slowly took my earbuds out once I arrived. Sofiane was running around his shop in what appeared to be a state of utter stress.

"Zizou, Zizou, it's happening so fast isn't it, little bro!" Sofiane said as I entered his shop.

He was sweating almost as much as he was smiling. His grin extended farther than I had ever seen before. I couldn't see past it into his broken soul. The smile was true. Sofiane was distracted to the point of pure bliss. Isn't that what everyone is chasing whether they are aware of it or not?

"My brother will be at the SeaTac airport to pick you up. Send him a message on Viber when you get there and let him know the number of the door that you are waiting at. He will pick you up in a grey Volkswagen Passat"

I nodded my head at Sofiane. I could sense there was something more that he was waiting to tell me. Only a few seconds later, I was proven right.

"Hey, little bro, come to the kitchen. I want to show you something."

I entered the kitchen. The smell of mayonnaise and merguez attacked my nostrils. On essentially every place that they could possibly be plastered, photographs of Sofiane and my father shone like diamonds in reflection of the bright light bulbs above us. I could see pictures from every *Ramadan*. Every barbeque.

Every birthday. Every soccer game. Every chillingly nostalgic night from years that had passed long ago.

"He was my best friend". Sofiane's eyes were covered in a thick coat of tears.

Soon my eyes were just a reflection of his. My vision got more and more blurry with every photograph I gazed at.

"We were meant to grow up together. This isn't what was supposed to happen. Mohamed wasn't supposed to die. Mohamed wasn't supposed to become a monster. He was meant to be the person he always was - my best friend - forever."

Sofiane collapsed onto his knees and looked to the stained ceiling. I stood beside him. My eyes were sealed shut. I couldn't bear the moment that I was in.

"You have to live your life to the fullest, Zizou," Sofiane said while staring at the floor.

Sofiane continued in a dramatic tone, "Restore your name. Create your own destiny, whatever it may be. But when you go the United States - you promise me you won't forget where you come from. You promise me you won't forget your father. You won't forget what has shaped you. This is who you are. You are Zinedine Zenoud, and that is your father. That is the way things have always been, and that's how they always will be. Promise me you'll remember who you are inch'Allah."

"I promise."

I finally opened my eyes as I said it. I got Sofiane off the mucky floor of his kitchen and hugged him. I hugged him as hard as I could. As we started to exit, he grabbed a photo from his collection.

"This was us in '94". Sofiane let out a chuckle. "We were both fifteen. It was late in the summer. Your dad had just gotten his first kiss and he wouldn't stop talking about it! Haha. Our families were on a trip to Oran, and we stayed out looking at the Mediterranean at night talking about what we were gonna do once we made it rich. That's when your grandfather came out and took this picture," he explained with recollection filling his baritone voice.

"I want you to take it with you to the United States. Take it with you - and when times get hard, look at it and think of us". Sofiane looked in my eyes with pure intent.

As per usual, I had to reject any gift out of respect, "Oh no Sofiane, I can't take this precio-"

He cut me off. "Zizou. Take it."

He opened my left hand with his right hand and used his left to put it in the palm of my hand.

"*Shokran amu*" I said to him.

Sofiane gave me a warm smile, "Alright little bro, let's head to your place. We gotta go to the airport soon."

When we returned to the apartment, my grandfather was already prepared to go.

"Ibrahim's father will drive us all to the airport. He will be here soon." My grandfather said once greeting us.

I started to wander around the apartment. There wasn't much to see, but to me, this place was everything. I opened the run down door to my room. I looked inside for a split second. I told myself that I would be back, that this couldn't be the last ever time I looked at that haunting room. I knew I couldn't promise myself that, but it was easier on my soul making promises I couldn't keep than actually exposing the truth.

"*Aduwah* Zizou, he is here. Let's go." My grandfather spoke from the other room.

I took one last glance into the room prior to lugging my suitcase to the front door. I was the last one out. I closed the creaky front door one final time. I reassured myself that I would return someday.

I hopped into Ibrahim's coal grey van. His dad was behind the wheel and Ibrahim was in the front seat. In the back sat the rest of the crew. My grandfather, Sofiane and I filled the remaining seats. The vehicle cruised through the crowded streets. The radio was blank. The silence was a subtle reminder to look around the van. To see all of my friends. To see my grandfather. To see Sofiane. To never forget this moment for the rest of my life.

"You ready bro"? Mamadou asked with a smile.

"Ready as I'll ever be". I replied, grinning back.

When we got to Charles de Gaulle, it felt like any warm summer day in Paris. I was relapsing on hedonistic nostalgia. It was all happening so fast. Looking back, I could not have understood what was occurring. I wasn't ready to understand. Two days previously, I was in a prison cell. Now, I was getting on a plane preparing to fly across the world, to a city I'd never been to. I was attempting to comprehend something outside my tragic condition. I wasn't ready to. I was just a boy. I couldn't have understood how empty and heartbroken I would feel. Despite all that, do I have any regrets? Not at all. I would do everything exactly the same if I could do it all over again.

I shared a hug with every single one of them. I looked blissfully towards the bright blue sky. I tied the laces on my ash grey shoes as water laced my sparkling eyes. I was entering a state of delirium. I don't even remember the last goodbye or walking through the airport. I can't remember getting stopped at every possible place they could stop me. All I can remember is finally stepping onto that plane. Strolling onto the aircraft knowing that I took my last breath of the musky Parisian air for a while.

I paced through the aisle and took my seat in the back of the aircraft. I was by the fogged up window. An American college student sat next to me. It took only a few minutes after the plane took off before he chatted me up. He was fluent in French, so it wasn't difficult to communicate.

"What are you doing flying to Seattle?" He said with a warm smile.

If my grandfather taught me anything, it was to be private and discrete.

"Just visiting family who moved there a few years ago, and you?" I replied.

He took a deep breath. As he exhaled, his core shook. It seemed as if his very being was empty, lacking everything except torment, affliction and misery. Misery filled that breath to the brim.

"I go to university at Sorbonne, but I grew up in Kirkland, right outside of Seattle. I wasn't gonna head back home until later in the summer, but my girl left me a week ago and she goes to University of Washington. We have been friends since I was 13. We have been together for 3 years. It is simply too urgent for me to wait any longer. I am driving myself insane in Paris. I have to go relapse on some nostalgia if you know what I mean?"

He let out a slightly forced laugh at the end of his paragraph. I didn't know exactly how to reply, but I could tell he just wanted someone to talk to. I was shocked that he felt the need to relay so many details to me. I wasn't someone that tended to immediately command the trust of strangers.

"Why'd she leave you?" I replied to him.

"She said something felt off. She told me that she didn't know if we could ever fix that. I understand. I would rather have her tell me the truth instead of continuing the facade. It just hurts," he choked out.

I patted him on the back. His head was in his hands. A silence followed before he picked up again.

"It's just…how could she leave so abruptly? After everything? She has been there for everything. My first kiss when I was 14 years old? She was the first person I called. When I got into Sorbonne? Who did I call? When I traveled the world and my thoughts kept me up at night, who did I call? She told me she'd be there forever. I can't blame her for not feeling as strongly as I do. I don't blame her for anything. I can't control her emotions. It just stings. It stings so strongly."

Tears dripped out of his bright, blank and broken blue eyes.

"The worst part is that she wants our friendship back. I can't be friends with her. I can't because I am so blatantly in love with her. I can't be friends with her and I can't see myself go through life without her there. I probably won't even see her when I go back for these next few weeks. I think I just need to get some perspective. I really don't know what I need. I'm agonized and she appears to be fine. Did she ever really care or was this all just a phase for her? Either way, I promised her I'd be there for her. Forever. I will hold myself to that. Is that the right choice to make? I don't know, but any other choice feels far too wrong."

He finally sat back up with a bright red face and puffy eyelids.

I finally replied and attempted to console him, "It's gonna be ok. You'll be ok. She will be ok. You have to believe that it will be ok. You can't regret anything. What's your name?"

"Anthony," he replied.

"Anthony, in my religion, we believe in fate. We are of the opinion that all of time has already been predetermined, and that we are subject to the manifestation of that destiny. Because of that destiny, here you sit. On an airplane home, to attempt to recapture happiness. If she cares about you, she'll understand. If she doesn't understand, then she wasn't meant to understand. That's disenchanting, I know. Trust me, I know. Maybe not with a girl - but you could never guess why I have to be on this flight right now. I put my pain down to fate," I stated.

Anthony looked me right into my dark, heartless eyes, "fate hurts."

He closed his eyes and let out a laugh. I laughed too. We stayed silent for a while, taking in the stuffy airplane oxygen, before Anthony finally got the nerve to ask me,

"So now you got me curious, it isn't family, is it? What's some Arab teenager from Paris doing flying to Seattle alone?"

He spilled out his soul to me. I thought he deserved to know at least some of the truth.

"I went to jail last year, and I just got out. My schooling is over in France and so is my soccer career. My family friend lives in Seattle and has a connection to a team here. I'm coming over to live with him and try to pursue my purpose. I come with the intent of playing soccer - but we know how that goes. I'm just searching for something that might fill the void that plagues me in Paris."

Anthony let out a sigh and looked past me out my window. He was still shaking.

"I'm sorry kid. What's your name, anyways?"

"Zinedine."

He struggled to hold in a smile, "Named after Zidane, eh?"

He laughed. I gave him a smile.

"What are you listening to in those headphones?"

"Just some French rap. How about you?" I replied.

"The Weeknd, of course. No other music has made any sense for the last week."

We traded headphones. His were much nicer than mine, but he didn't seem to care. In his ears was a muffled tracking of PNL's latest release, "A l'ammoniaque,"

Why did this small flower wither?
She was so pretty, far from the jungle
But hey, the jungle caught up with her

...

Where I'm from, we love you and then we forget you
Where I'm from, we bleed and then we grow up

...

I'm becoming someone in order to exist
Because nobody invited us

...

The angels are sad, the demons love it
Why did you say "I love you" randomly?
We're full of sorrow behind our claws
I waited patiently to feel myself live
Give me time

...

While tomorrow intoxicates me

Then the desolate hook came back, and even though I couldn't hear it, I knew exactly where the track was by the look on his face, which was full of fury and sorrow.

I love you
Yeah, yeah, yeah, yeah, yeah
Madly
Yeah, yeah, yeah, yeah, yeah, yeah
Passionately
Yeah, yeah, yeah, yeah, yeah
With ammonia

In my headphones was "Wicked Games" by The Weeknd. He wrote down the French translation for me, along with his phone number and a note saying to contact him if I ever need anything. Despite the obvious erotic nature of the track, that is not the way my mind interpreted the vibe or even lyrics.

Mjtufo, nb, J'mm hjwf zpv bmm J hpu
Hfu nf pgg pg uijt, J offe dpogjefodf jo nztfmg
Mjtufo, nb, J'mm hjwf zpv bmm pg nf
Hjwf nf bmm pg ju, J offe bmm pg ju up nztfmg
Tp ufmm nf zpv mpwf nf

...

Fwfo uipvhi zpv epo'u mpwf nf
Kvtu ufmm nf zpv mpwf nf
(J'mm hjwf zpv xibu J offe, J'mm hjwf zpv bmm pg nf)
Fwfo uipvhi zpv epo'u mpwf nf

From my perspective, Abel Tesfaye was singing his sorrows to the world, whether it made sense or not. For Anthony, every letter that the Canadian-Ethiopian singer belted out was about his girl, whether it made sense or not. When I heard the woeful words, I saw a world that clearly did not love me. All I wanted was for the world to want me as much as I wanted the world. I desperately needed the world to give me the confidence that I desired. I would give anything and everything for a taste of that. Just as Anthony would give anything for the love that he cannot seem to let go of. We would both give everything to fill the inexplicable and unexplainable emptiness inside our hearts.

I pulled out the photo of my dad and Sofiane when they were younger as the lugubrious track faded. My dad smiled, and his eyes twinkled in the Saharan moonlight. Sofiane was full of pure joy, and his innocent hope for the future emanated throughout time. The stars were shining on them. The warm, crisp, summer air was alive. I could still feel it.

I closed my eyes and I saw everything. I wished more than anything that it would just be dark, but it wasn't. It never is.

Chapter 7: Runaway: October 22, 2018

I've been in Redmond, Washington, for two months. It was a little way away from the main city of Seattle, but already I have begun to notice the differences between here and home. It was almost the opposite of Paris. You could walk anywhere in Seattle and the air would be fresher than the most spectacular gardens and markets back home. There are gigantic pine trees as far as your eye can see. Cold rain perennially pours from the grey sky into the lakes and puddles, blurring your crystal clear reflection in the freshwater.

Just as was arranged in Barbés, I live with Sofiane's younger brother, Zakaria. He has been incredibly kind ever since the moment that he picked me up from the airport. Zakaria looks and acts just enough like Sofiane to make me feel like I am at home for the slightest of moments, however, he is just different enough to almost immediately snatch that recollection away from me. The apartment complex we live in is called the Delson Apartments. It is a pleasant property situated about a half an hour from the Space Needle, and about twenty minutes from where my team trains. I stay in the smallest of the 3 bedrooms. Zakaria's 7-year-old son Ilyas lives adjacent to me, with Zakaria and his wife Zahia having the largest room across the unit.

Everything is unimaginably different here. The demographics. The customer service. The food. The *soccer.* Most of the time it feels like the 4 of us are the only Algerians in this entire state. I eat almost all of my meals at home and spend almost all of my free time on the field. I truly enjoy shopping discount clothing at the *Ross Dress for Less* right outside our apartment. That store is honestly the best part of America so far.

I speak to my grandfather on the phone every day. He has always wanted to visit America. I often ring him on video chat and show him around the area. The part he's been most fascinated with so far is the Masjid down the street from me. The Muslim Association of the Puget Sound, or MAPS as everyone calls it, is situated within walking distance of Delson. Beneath the overwhelming display of greenery lies a beautiful marble Mosque. The inside is absolutely stunning, covered entirely with precisely stained tiles, divine Arabic inscriptions, and incredible Islamic architecture. Masses gather for every Friday prayer. They run from their automobiles to the grand, maroon doors in an effort to avoid the drizzling rain which is almost always present. Most of the Muslims at MAPS are either Egyptian or East African, however there are minorities of almost every kind. Indonesians, Pakistanis, Chinese, American Converts, Middle Easterners and even Maghrebis can be spotted in the crowds every Friday.

My grandfather's admiration for the Masjid has influenced me to spend more time there than I probably would have on my own. I go to every *Jummah Salat*, and then go kick around at the Marymoor Soccer Fields which are right next to the Masjid. Sometimes, a group of older guys from a Chinese Church in the area come and join me. None of us can form a coherent sentence in English, but we communicate with the ball. That's a language that we are all fluent in.

My team, which is called O.S.A.F.C, trains three times a week at Starfire Soccer Complex. The facility is in a town called Tukwila. My first few training sessions were nerve racking to say the least. My coaches name is Stuart Hill. He's an older, pale man from Manchester. He has white hair and a stocky build. Coach Stu played over 20 years professionally, most notably for European super club, Manchester City.

Mr. Hill's methods are definitely not easy, but they are undoubtedly effective. Zakaria took me to my first practice in August. He introduced me to Coach Stuart and helped translate the coaching instructions for me. The first thing Stu had me do was run what he liked to call *Killers*, which are basically amped up versions of your classical suicide runs. By the end of my first set, my vomit was all over the 3G turf pitch. Stuart felt little sympathy.

"I've heard all the noises. I've seen all the faces. You can't fool me! Keep running!" He yelled emphatically as I slowed down.

I kept myself going. Those first few trainings were incredibly rigorous, but extremely rewarding. It didn't take long before performing a Killer was totally manageable. Stuart describes me as an "extremely gifted player with no brain." He often tells me that I have the technical ability to play at elite levels, but need to drastically improve my decision making, and especially my emotional stability on the pitch. I have a temper, and it rages in the face of defeat. According to Stuart, the only Zinedine who can pull off a temper is Zidane himself.

My reasoning for reacting the way I do is embedded in the fact that I traveled across the globe for this opportunity. I can't stand to watch any game, training, or opportunity pass me by without taking full advantage. Stu tells me that I need to find a way to use this as motivation instead of letting it feed my rage. He is absolutely right, but it's irrefutably grueling to accept. Every day I get closer to solving it, and some days it seems completely corrected, until I fixate my attention on a small detail and internally infuriate myself over it until I cannot hold in my emotions any longer. Once that occurs, it feels as if the process starts all over again.

Zakaria and his wife both work long hours, and I am not allowed to drive yet, so I carpool with a middle aged Egyptian man who I met at the Masjid named Ahmed. Ahmed lives in Tukwila and works for Microsoft in Redmond. He finishes work every day an hour before my training, so he swings by Delson and picks me up, before dropping me off at fields on his way home. After training, a teammate of mine who lives near me drops me back off at the apartment. I creak open the door every twilight and say *Salam U Alaikum*, just as I always did in Barbés. Just as I will always do for the rest of my life.

There is always an airy feeling around the apartment. The emotion extends past the white walls of our living quarters and into the rest of the Greater Seattle Area. There is a certain, unfathomably distinct peacefulness found in the nature of strolling down the damp, grey sidewalk beneath the shadows of evergreen trees.

Usually Zahia makes an Algerian dish for the family and leaves out the leftovers for me as I get home after the family eats dinner. I heat them up in the microwave and speak softly with Zakaria and Zahia about whatever comes to mind. We swig small glasses of mint tea in an uncharacteristically American fashion. We reminisce on the past. I let my instinct carry myself through each and every day, because if I become weary and start to let myself ponder the nature of my abstruse condition, I drift into a state of uncontrollable despair.

The truth is that Redmond is far too serene for me to correctly oblige to societal standards. I wander through the streets alone and there is an eldritch, discernable lack of blazing frequencies that hinder me from properly pondering perspective. I wince at the thought of anything beyond my scope of control. The humanity that supervises my soul simply won't allow a lack of comprehension to trigger reward centers in my fragile mind. Understanding that you can never understand is the most intolerable torment that our existence has to offer. It trumps all imaginable sentiments. Love is nothing when you understand it doesn't matter. Pain is nothing when you understand it doesn't matter. *The World is Nothing* when you understand that it can't possibly matter. We stop ourselves from coming to these conclusions because we were never meant to let this form of trauma feast on our very being. Instinct is our natural barrier between reality and sorrow. We see everything through enigmatically rose tinted lenses.

Unfortunately, my prescription seems to have expired. I have enough time, silence and intellect to take everything into heartbreaking consideration. Our dreams will never be fulfilled.

If they are, they will never be anything more than a phenomenal distraction from the fact that our dreams cannot be defined as relevant in any possible interpretation of the term. Ignorance truly is bliss. That's why we artificially instigate ignorance at any chance we get. Ignorance is a prescription that none of us explicitly asked for, but we all so desperately need.

Last Friday night, I was eating dinner at home with the family. We usually have very quiet meals, and this one was not any different. Ilyas chimed in with an allegory from his school day, everyone pretended to be deeply invested in it, and we all got on with our meal. It was just another day. After finishing our eloquent chicken dish, Zakaria called me to join him outside. We strolled out into the fresh, moist breeze underneath a familiar lack of celestial bodies. Zakaria struck a chord with his subject of discussion in between puffs of his Marlboro Cigarette.

"I know we have tried to keep your family history lowkey, but I guess word gets out."

He had an uncomfortable look on his face. I stayed silent.

"A couple who lives downtown were in Paris during the attacks. They survived, but their 24-year-old son was killed. They hit my line yesterday after hearing from someone at MAPS that you were living with me. They would really like to meet you, just to exchange perspective. They didn't seem bitter or to have sinister intentions. I think it could benefit you to truly understand. You are old enough and mature enough. But it's your choice of course *habibi*."

He playfully swiped at my ink black hair with his leathery Algerian hands and let out an undeniably forced chuckle. He was right. It was time for me to attempt to understand just what my parents did.

"Are they available next week?" I replied.

He looked into my empty eyes and hacked out an excess of smoke, which immediately struck my olfactory organs. A sense of nostalgia overwhelmed the dopamine receptors in my brain. It smelled like home. Soon enough, I was beaming. What a phenomenal distraction.

Chapter 8: Zizou: November 19, 2018

After an agonizing month of waiting, the older couple and I had finally arranged a time to meetup and discuss their near death experience from almost fifteen years ago. Zakaria offered to come along with me, but I told him that this was always the type of thing that I wanted to go into alone. Over the years, I have slowly but surely begun to understand how unique my perspective truly is. Unlike most teenagers plagued by dread, a Google search won't uncover any articles regarding my place in the world. Being the son of some of the most Mephistophelian individuals our modern, globalized society has ever seen is absolutely an incredibly isolated position.

The couple was very precise on what they wanted, which was to invite me over to join them for dinner. I proposed that we meet downtown for coffee or lunch, but they insisted that they were to welcome me into their home. As I was getting ready to head out of the apartment, I asked Zakaria why they were so dead set on having me over to their house, which was located in West Seattle.

"They told me they wanted to kill the tension and stigma early on. Are you sure you don't want me to come, Zizou?" He seemed unsure and uneasy, flickering his eyelashes and scratching his scruffy goatee.

"No, it's fine Zak, but *shokran.*"

I put on black jeans and a matching plaid shirt that I had bought from Ross when I first got to America. I took one last glance in the silver mirror, doing everything I could to make sure I didn't strike even the slightest memory of my father. I combed my hair to the other side. I shaved any facial hair that was still lingering on my familiar face. Nothing worked. Frustration filled the void in my frozen soul.

I opened our noticeably silent front door. We got in Zakaria's grey, stick shift Passat and started rolling through the streets. Time was moving forward, but it felt as if we were turning back the years more and more with every mile we drove towards the couple's house. Zakaria was in charge of the Soundtrack, and was humming along to "American Terrorist", an older track from Chicago rapper Lupe Fiasco. I didn't take in the lyrical content of the track at the time, mostly because I still only spoke survival English. Looking back, the words were chillingly fitting,

> Dbnpvgmbhfe Upsbit, Cjcmft boe hmpsjpvt Rv'sbot
> Uif cpplt uibu ublf zpv up ifbwfo boe mfu zpv nffu uif
> Mpse uifsf
> Ibwf cfdpnf njtjoufsqsfufe, sfbtpot gps xbsgbsf
> Xf sfbe 'fn xjui cmjoe fzft, J hvbsbouff zpv uifsf't npsf
> uifsf

We merged onto the Evergreen Point Floating Bridge, which was outstretched over Lake Washington. The deep blue water shone under the milky, emotionless twilight. I looked on past the irrelevant activities of the blind masses, instead towards the towering pine trees and clouded, murky sunset. Countless vehicles drove past us and we drove past countless vehicles. Each of us with our own past, unlikely to ever intersect. We will simultaneously wander through the daily motions of life, urging ourselves on to pursue the pleasure of tomorrow.

We eventually got to the neighborhood. An apocalyptic vibe dispersed through the air outside the car. The frigid, autumn breeze whispered in my ear as I opened the passenger door of the Passat. Bright yellow lights poured through the windows of all the houses on the shadowed street. Something was chillingly familiar about that specific moment.

"Ok, Zizou, their names are Samuel and Alexandra Wilson. Their son's name was Nathan. They are both American but they lived in France for over 25 years. Be as polite as you can be and be careful. Call me if you need anything. I will be nearby. Salam."

"Salam Zak."

I gently closed the car door and started on my way to the front door with goosebumps covering my rough skin. I placed my shivering finger on the doorbell. I closed my eyes and paused for a few seconds, before mindlessly clicking the button.

Samuel opened the door. He had straight white hair and round prescription glasses covering his hazel eyes. He gave me a warm smile, and then a firm handshake.

"Zinedine, you made it. It's nice to meet you!" he said in a clear tone.

He proceeded to politely welcome me in. I looked around the place. It was extremely neat and well put together. A hushed, relaxed Pandora radio station was playing on the television. Mrs. Wilson was sitting on the couch sipping her coffee. Once she saw me, she urged herself to stand up. She slipped on her pair of pink sliders and approached me without saying a word. My stomach began to jump. A million possibilities ran through my head. I instinctively closed my eyes as she got closer. I could feel myself quivering. She hugged me. She didn't let go for what felt like ages.

She spoke as softly as the songs that were flowing through the tightly-knit atmosphere of the home. "Come on, let's have dinner."

We all took our seats at the table. A woman who appeared to be in her early thirties came downstairs and joined us at the table. Mr. Wilson set the dish of spaghetti on the table.

"Don't worry Zinedine - I made sure these meatballs don't have any pork in them," he said as he took his seat at the table.

"Thank you so much for your kindness." I replied in a state of pleasant shock.

Mr. Wilson proceeded to introduce me to his daughter, who had already been awkwardly sitting at the table with me for a few moments.

"This is our daughter Lauren. She comes over for dinner on many nights each week. She is a clinical psychologist in Tacoma."

I shook hands with Lauren. She had pink glasses covering her eyes, which were a color that I couldn't exactly put my finger on. Upon looking into them, I received an intense stare. I felt as if she was psychologically assessing me, even though I was just meeting her for the first time. It wasn't aggressive or judgmental, it was just a bit distressing. I wasn't sure if I wanted anyone to get a glimpse of my true colors. I wasn't sure what my true colors even were, and I'm terrified of the possibilities. I was absolutely stunned at how welcoming the Wilsons were. My father murdered their son. I expected at least some underlying despair and angst towards me - but there wasn't anything at all. I felt like part of the family.

We began to commence conversation as we ate the delicious Italian meal. "So Zinedine, what brought you to Seattle? Zakaria told us on the phone that you are here living with him but he didn't give many details."

I could feel my Maghrebi intuition telling me not to give many details - but they deserved my story. There was an energy in the room that simply could not be mistaken. It's the type of atmosphere that can remain with you for a long time.

"I was raised by my grandfather, my dad's father. Over a year ago, I was walking through our neighborhood when a family member of one of the victims started to assault me. I foolishly punched back, which sent me to prison for 12 months. When I got out in July, my opportunities in France were non-existent.

Luckily, I got the chance to come live with Zakaria - who is a family friend," I explained.

They listened closely and nodded their heads at the words I was saying. Mrs. Wilson replied in a caring tone.

"That must've been a lot for you - being in prison. Especially considering your family history. What was it like?"

I finished my mouthful of pasta.

"It was unimaginable. Part of me feels like it never happened. I saw so much. I learned so much. I am shocked I made it out of there alive and in an acceptable state of mind. You probably know that my father went to prison for petty crime, and that he was radicalized in prison. It would have been so easy for me to fall to the same ill willed promises. Once you're in the environment, the outside world becomes irrelevant. Losing your mind in the radicalization and regret is easier than anyone on the outside could ever imagine."

"I'm sorry you had to go through that, Zinedine. Our world is unforgiving. Everything can change in a flash." Mr. Wilson stated in a truly caring tone.

A jagged bolt of pain and guilt struck my heart. There I was receiving sympathy from a couple who lost their son due to my father. I didn't feel like I deserved it. I felt extreme guilt at my very presence. I began to shift the topic; focusing on my sorrow felt selfish and shameful. I took a deep breath and hopped onto a train of thought that had been pulling at my soul since I had heard that they wanted to meet with me.

"Mr. Wilson, Mrs. Wilson, Lauren - I am so sorry. I am so unbelievably sorry. I am so sorry my parents did what they did. I resent it. I resent them. I wish we could turn back time and change fate. I wish it didn't have to be this way. I'm so sorry," I choked out the words, trying not to let any of the water escape my evil eyes.

Mr. Wilson turned my words around in his head for a minute before formulating his response.

"You couldn't have changed anything. You didn't choose this. Please don't apologize. We didn't have you over because we wanted you to apologize, or to pile stress onto your already heavy heart. We wanted you to come because we wanted to get to know you. We want to understand the story from your perspective. All four of us have something in common; we wake up every day and regret the same events with the same amount of sadness."

I displayed the best smile I could give. Mrs. Wilson smiled back at me.

"If you don't mind, I would love to hear about your son." I said to her.

"You never expect to bury your son. You expect to bury your parents, maybe an older sibling, maybe a spouse," she giggled and nudged Mr. Wilson.

"Hey!" He laughed back.

The aforementioned solitude mood immediately returned, "but you never expect to bury your son. You never expect that those 'goodbyes' and 'good mornings' were the last that he would ever say to you. You never expect to see his daughter grow up without him. You never expect him to leave this world before you do," she said in a mature yet vulnerable tone.

Lauren decided to chime in, ""I was 17 when my brother died. If there was one defining characteristic of his personality, it was his optimism. To him, the glass was always half full - no matter how empty it truly could have been. If he would have survived, he would've been delighted to meet you and understand things from your perspective."

Mrs. Wilson nodded her head in agreement. She took a sip of water before continuing where her daughter left off.

"He died from a gunshot to the head. At least he didn't have to suffer, and it went quickly."

She took a deep breath, preparing herself to recall the misery.

"We were out having dinner. All of a sudden, we heard blood curdling screams adjacent to the bullets flying through the air. The entire restaurant ducked. Unfortunately, a shot hit Nate. We knew right away. His cheerfulness had vacated our world. We laid on the floor next to him pretending to be dead. Luckily for us, we managed to escape alive. Leaving him there was the hardest thing I have ever done. Nothing will ever erase that image from my head. For years, it was all I saw when I closed my eyes."

She exhaled. She could once again close her mind.

"Nathan had a 2-year-old daughter at the time named Scarlett. Her mother is a French-Moroccan lady that Nathan went to school with. She is your age now and lives with her mother in Marseille. It is hard for them to be in Paris. She is in Seattle visiting us right now, but she is out with her friends."

She politely implied that Scarlett knew that I was going to meet with her grandparents but rejected the chance at any interaction with me. Mrs. Wilson was starting to tear up. Mr. Wilson maintained his composure and decided to speak. Lauren looked up to the chandelier directly above us, appearing to make an effort to faze her mind out of focus.

"I'm sure that most, including yourself, categorize your parents as monsters above anything. This is a fair assessment at surface value. However, being there, there was a crystal clear energy that night, and it wasn't hatred. It was fear. Your father's arm shook rapidly with every bullet he released, and by the end of it all he was repeatedly screaming out "astaghfirullah, astaghfirullah!" before taking his own life. Your mother tried to calm him down, stating that they had completed their task. She seemed much more cold-hearted than your father, as if it was always her intention to use him to manifest her twisted agenda. He screamed ferociously at her, stating that they had tampered with fate. He repented too late. He had already used too many clips for the world to ever forgive him, and more importantly too

82

many clips to ever forgive himself. He knew that those moments had to be the last ones that he was to experience. It still feels like a clouded nightmare, but I remember it all so vividly. I remember hearing your father wail before activating his suicide vest right outside of the restaurant where we laid - playing dead with our son lying next to us."

Tears streamed down my fearful face. Mrs. Wilson gave me another hug, even longer than the first. I didn't know what to say except that I was sorry. They told me that it was going to be okay. I wanted so badly to believe them, but I didn't know if I really could. As per usual, my visual senses faded away. I felt the effects of agony, reverting to my instinctive desire to distract myself from reality. The Pandora station was still playing in the background. I tuned my mind into the music for the entirety of the upcoming track. It was "The Moth & The Flame", by Les Deux Love Orchestra.

Uif npui epo'u dbsf xifo if tfft uif gmbnf
If njhiu hfu cvsofe, cvu if't jo uif hbnf
Boe podf if't jo, if dbo'u hp cbdl
If'mm cfbu ijt xjoht ujmm if cvsot uifn cmbdl

Op, uif npui epo'u dbsf xifo if tfft uif gmbnf
Op, uif npui epo'u dbsf xifo if tfft uif gmbnf

Uif npui epo'u dbsf jg uif gmbnf jt sfbm
'Dbvtf gmbnf boe uif npui hpu b txffuifbsu efbm
Boe opuijoh gvfmt b hppe gmjsubujpo
Mjlf offe boe bohfs boe eftqfsbujpo

Op, uif npui epo'u dbsf jg uif gmbnf jt sfbm

Op, uif npui epo'u dbsf jg uif gmbnf jt sfbm

Tp dpnf po, mfu't hp, sfbez ps opu
'Dbvtf uifsf't b gmbnf J lopx, ipuufs uibo ipu
Boe xjui b gvtf uibu't tp uipspvhimz tipu
(Bxbz)

Uif npui epo'u dbsf jg uif gmbnf cvsot mpx
'Dbvtf uif npui cfmjfwft jo bo bgufshmpx
Boe gmbnft bsf ofwfs epvtfe dpnqmfufmz
Bmm zpv sfbmmz offe jt uif mpwf pg ifbu

Op, uif npui epo'u dbsf jg uif gmbnf cvsot mpx
Op, uif npui epo'u dbsf jg uif gmbnf cvsot mpx

My humanity obfuscated the remainder of the evening. Before I knew it, I was back at Delson. I laid there in my bed, staring at the spinning fan. It was dawn in Paris. I decided to call my grandfather. The phone rang a couple times before he answered.

"*Salam Djidda,* how's home?"

He sighed, and then replied. "It's home, you know." He chuckled.

"I just went to an American couple's house for dinner. They lost their son in the attacks, and they were there too but survived. They were very polite and treated me like family."

"That's good. Good to know there are forgiving people in the world," my grandfather vaguely said.

He didn't want to go into things too deeply - instead giving me a typical surface level response.

"I'm so sorry that my dad's life took the course that it did. I am so sorry *Djiddah*. I can't imagine how hard that was for you."

He took the same deep breath that Mrs. Wilson did, "There is nothing that can prepare you for that. There is nothing that can save you afterwards. There is nothing. Nothing."

I knew he didn't want to go any further.

"Have a great day *Djiddah*."

"Sleep well Zizou. See you soon *inch-Allah*"
I dropped the phone onto the floor. "Growing Pains III" by American rapper Logic soothed my psychotic state. My whole body buzzed with anxious dread. The music eventually faded to oblivion as I closed my eyes.

J hvftt nbzcf J xbt uijoljoh uijoht xpvme cf ejggfsfou opx
Dbvtf xifo J xblf vq nz esfbnt gbef

Fwfszuijoh dbtdbef

Jo uijt wbojmmb tlz, J gffm mjlf Ebwje Bbnft

Xiz nvtu J pqfo nz fzft?

J xjti uibu J dpvme tubz btmffq gpsfwfs

Buubjo fwfsz hpbm J xboufe boe xbudi ju sfqfbu gpsfwfs

Xjmm ju ibqqfo, nbzcf ofwfs

Nbzcf tp, J hpu up lopx

Cvu ufmm nf xiz?

J qjduvsf nztfmg bu uif upq cvu J lopx uibu J'n esfbnjoh

Xjmm J xblf vq cfgpsf J gjobmmz dpogspou bmm nz efnpot?

Nbzcf opu

Bmm J lopx jt uijt mjgf J mjwf J dbo'u mjwf ju op mpohfs

Xjti J xbt tuspohfs, xjti uibu J dpvme tvswjwf

Uvso po uif UW mfu ju xbti nz csbjo

Qsfufoe uibu gbnjmz't nz gbnjmz up bwpje uif qbjo

Ifmmp dijmesfo, ipx xbt tdippm?

Ju xbt hppe, ipx 'cpvu zpv?

J mpwf zpv (J mpwf zpv tpo)

J mpwf nbnb upp

Bsf zpv sfbez gps ejoofs? J'n bcmf up tfu uif ubcmf

Ujmm J tobq pvu uif gbcmf xifo uibu UW uvso pgg

boe J sfbmjaf J'n cbdl jo ifmm

Chapter 9: Le Ciel Est La Limite: January 4th, 2019

Coach Stuart's training regimen has only gotten more and more physically demanding as time has gone on, but I have learnt to appreciate it. I have a great deal of respect for the coach and my teammates. Many of them are of Sub Saharan African descent, while some are Italians who have been brought to the United States by the Mediterranean owners of the club. Despite the eccentric racial diversity on the team, there have been no problems regarding discrimination. I have received nothing but support from everyone in regard to my familial history. Being the youngest player on the team at 17 years old, I've been learning a lot from some of the older guys in the group. I am slowly but surely picking up English, thusly assimilating myself into American society.

Over the winter months, we have been coming together and scraping results. I have not been called upon in an official match yet, but I can feel myself gradually improving with every session. We are traveling to San Diego in two weeks to play in a showcase tournament against some American and Mexican teams.

My mid-season review with Coach Stuart is this afternoon. We have arranged to meet at a Starbucks in the nearby town of Sammamish to go over my player report and discuss my role in the upcoming games. The only time I could get a ride up to the Sammamish plateau was early in the morning, so I was dropped off multiple hours prior to my appointment. I put in my earbuds and wandered around the beautiful suburb. An abundance of greenery saturated the entirety of my peripheral vision. I eventually meandered into a nearby park and took a seat on the wooden dock that was situated on Pine Lake. Some older Southern Asian men were peacefully fishing in the greenish-turquoise lake. The air was void of stress and angst. The only thing that attempted to fill the free atmosphere was the chirps of the birds and overlapping flow of water and rap in my ears. I couldn't lay there for very long before I started to become psychotic. As per usual, there was nothing stopping me from putting everything into perspective. I swiftly stood up and started in the direction of Starbucks. I am required to pursue my hedonistic, instinctual desires in order to find contentment. There is no inner peace. The harder I try, the more realistically I see things. The more realistically I see things, the more desolate existence becomes. Distractions fuel me to find relevance in an irrelevant world. That is simply the way things are. The human condition doesn't offer another solution. If you think it does, you are properly distracted.

I didn't have to wait long at Starbucks before Stu arrived. He slowly strolled into the store and took a seat at the table. The fireplace was roaring next to us. Uninterested teenagers occupied the shop, visibly taking their modern American lifestyle for granted. Stuart opened proceedings in his gritty Mancunian accent.

"Zinedine, how've you been son?"

I gave him a firm handshake.

"Very well, and yourself coach?"

Further pleasantries were exchanged before Stuart and I got into the content of our rendezvous.

"Zizou, I am very pleased with your development so far this year. When you came to us you were what I like to classify as a 'street player' - a player who has honed his skills playing on the streets and not in a formal training environment. Sometimes it is hard to convert a street footballer into one capable of performing on the full field, but you are getting there. We still have a lot of work to do, but you have come leaps and bounds since the summer and I am extremely proud."

It was very relieving to get some positive reinforcement. Soccer was the reason I immigrated to the United States. I was delighted to know that I wasn't stagnating.

"Thank you, Coach."

Coach turned to focus on the mental side of the game.

"As for the mental side of the game, you still have a bit more room to grow. Your tactical awareness is not up to par to play at higher levels. This will come with more game experience."

Stuart took a slight pause.

"Our starting Right Winger is not able to travel to San Diego with the squad. You will be called upon to play in his spot. I will be counting on you to be an "x-factor" for our squad. I expect to see you taking on players, cutting onto that left foot of yours and taking shots. There will be some big-name scouts at this tournament, so make the most of this opportunity."

I was absolutely beaming. I was starting to bear the fruits of my hard work. This was my opportunity to impress.

"Thank you, Stu. I will not let you down."

"Sounds good lad. See you at training."

I exited the coffee shop with a swagger to my walk. "Zizou", A new track by MMZ that pays homage to my namesake Zinedine Zidane was blasting through my headphones.

And to me, my *zoo* is becoming kind of like Cali
I've been thinking about it for years
I don't wanna end up in prison...
We have the "It's never too late" mentality...
We came to take everything, no one gave us anything...
I know that you remember us, I know that you recognize us...
Yeah, homie, we're marked for life, that's what has allowed us to stand out

During the next week at training, I made sure to do everything I could to solidify my spot in the starting lineup. Competing with older men was never easy, but that struggle and my determination to overcome it was making me a better player each and every session. By the time we were headed to San Diego on the 17th, I was fully confident in my ability to make a memorable impression in Southern California.

I made my way through the Sea-Tac Airport in a surprisingly swift fashion, with only one round of questioning and a pat down at security. I put this down to the fact that I was traveling with a group of players, which made me less of a suspect. I closed my eyes and let my mind fade for the duration of the flight. Soon enough, we were amongst palm trees and saltwater.

I called my grandfather as soon as I got to the hotel room to let him know I made it to California safely. He told me to be cautious and to enjoy myself. I always appreciate speaking with my grandfather. I check up on him as often as I can. I worry about him living on his own, but I'm sure he feels the same way about me.

When you grow up in France, Southern California is continuously glamorized. Hollywood. The girls. The fashion. The music. It is always at the center of our attention. Now that I am actually here, none of it seems to matter to me. The only thing on my mind is the three matches we have this weekend. Our first match is against Albion SC, a local team with a fairly prestigious reputation in the American footballing community. The game on Saturday is against CF Tijuana, an amateur side from just across the Mexican border. Our third and final game is one that really captures my eye; a showdown with the Seattle Sounders under-23 team. The Seattle Sounders are one of the most successful professional soccer clubs in the United States. Like O.S.A.F.C, they train at Starfire Soccer Complex in Tukwila. I will be hoping to impress their coaching staff in our match against their U23 team.

The entire weekend was flowing around my foggy head. I tried to get some sleep. I knew that I needed it for the huge weekend that was finally upon me. I woke up in the morning with fresh legs. Despite a heavy wave of nervousness continuously crashing through me, I was raring to go. I made sure to eat a healthy breakfast at the hotel and hopped on the team van as soon as they let me. My teammates seemed unfazed at playing in the showcase, but they clearly noticed my nerves. On the ride to the game, an older teammate named Julius attempted to calm my impulsive energy.

"You're gonna do great kid. You have the talent. Just go out there and strut your stuff".

Although it didn't do much to shift my mentality, I really did appreciate his efforts, "Thanks Julius. Let's get out there and show them what we're made of."

We hopped out of the vans and made our way to the muddy, unkempt fields. After what seemed like a brisk warmup, my first match for O.S.A.F.C was underway.

The first 10 minutes of the match were choppy to say the least. The two teams seemed to be adjusting to the poor condition of the surface. Neither side was controlling the game for any significant portion of time. I had barely even touched the ball.

As we got closer to the end of the first half, we started to retain possession a little bit better. Despite the success of my team as a collective group, I was not shining on an individual level. My touch felt off, my legs felt heavy, and my mind was filled to the brim with stress. I lost the ball more times than I had kept it, and my teammates were growing weary at my poor performance.

In the last play before the end of the half, I received the ball on the halfway line. Attempting to make up for my poor match thus far, I decided to try to showcase some of my dribbling ability. After the first few touches, I was decked to the ground by the opposing defender. By the time I was able to get up and track back, Albion SC had already stuck the ball in the back of the net. The referee immediately blew the halftime whistle. Stuart chewed me apart in his half time team talk.

He screamed at me in front of my teammates, who were equally as livid as my experienced coach, "You aren't on the damn streets anymore! Pass the ball!"

I was substituted for the second half, and I watched from the freezing bench as my teammates succumbed to a 1-0 defeat.

Stuart let out his frustration to us at the end of the match.

"All it takes is one bloody mistake. One mistake lost you the match today."

Other players would feel angry at Stuart for villainizing them the way that he villainized me, but I was not mad at him at all. I was only mad at myself for squandering such an opportunity. Everything Stuart said was correct.

I was fuming when I returned to my hotel room. It was an almost inhuman rage. I looked in the blurry mirror at my criminal eyes, letting them be the window to my iniquitous soul. I ripped off my cleats and leaped onto the creaky hotel bed. I threw the rough pillows onto the floor and pounded my fists onto the cheap mattress. None of it made me feel any better.

Maybe football wasn't for me. Maybe I wasn't cut out for this profession. Deep down, I knew that wasn't true. I told myself that I needed time. It didn't take long before the world and everything within imagination became irrelevant once again. I began to shut down. I plugged in my earbuds and let the close-minded perspective of my own place in the human condition take over - just as it was designed to. The soul-stirring strings of legendary song "Stairway to Heaven" by Led Zeppelin distracted me just enough to remain sane.

Uifsf't b mbez xip't tvsf bmm uibu hmjuufst jt hpme
Boe tif't cvzjoh uif tubjsxbz up ifbwfo
Xifo tif hfut uifsf tif lopxt, jg uif tupstf bsf bmm dmptfe
Xjui b xpse tif dbo hfu xibu tif dbnf gps
Ppi, ppi, boe tif't cvzjoh uif tubjsxbz up ifbwfo
Uifsf't b tjho po uif xbmm cvu tif xbout up cf tvsf
'Dbvtf zpv lopx tpnfujnft xpset ibwf uxp nfbojoht
Jo b usff cz uif csppl, uifsf't b tpohcjse xip tjoht
Tpnfujnft bmm pg pvs uipvhiut bsf njthjwfo

94

The lyricism really does make me wonder. These inapplicable whereabouts of my mind were enough of an antidote for the time being. I knew that it was destined to gradually fade away.

I was ready to shift my limited focus towards the match. It wasn't an option to perform poorly against Tijuana FC. Ever since I had met with the Wilson's, an immense amount of pressure flowed through me. I felt hundreds of souls occupying the place of mine, all searching for the same sense of fulfillment. I felt as if they lived on with me - and it was my responsibility to succeed for them. Failure simply wasn't an option. My existence in this world is directly tied to the harrowing, offbeat massacre. Whether I like it or not, that fact will forever be part of me. They will forever live on through me, until my day to join them comes *inch-Allah*.

There was a solitude feeling as we approached our field the next afternoon for our second match of the showcase. The pressure I felt remained, and in a sense, grew to even more intense levels. My shoulders felt locked in place, afraid to an extent that made it impossible for them to move in any direction. As I had expected, Stuart dropped me from the starting lineup for the match. It made sense - and I had no qualms with his decision. All that was on my mind was the winning goal I knew I would inevitably score once I was brought on.

The Mexican style of soccer reminded me of how North Africans in France approach the game. They played with a flair-induced tactic, reliant on the individualistic talent of their players. It was exactly like watching Algerians play back in Barbés. They were willing to give anything to win, not just for themselves, but for each other. Every match was a war. The Latin vibe brought me back to France and made me internally reflect on what makes me a special player. I had to be willing to give anything to win, not just for myself, but for everyone who has gotten me to the point where I am and to everyone who will have gotten me the places I was destined to go.

The first half ended 0-0, but Tijuana were dominating the match. Our fullbacks did not know how to contain the pace of the tricky Hispanic wingers. With around 20 minutes remaining in the game, Stuart called my name. I leapt up from the bench and went straight to him. He put his arm around my shoulder and whispered instructions in my ear.

"You are gonna go on the right wing. These defenders are strong, but they love to dive in. Use your agility and be one step ahead of them. I expect you to make a difference. I expect you to make up for yesterday. There are grown men sitting on that bench next to you who won't see a minute of action today, despite the fact that they didn't screw up yesterday. I am calling on you because I have full faith in you to fix your error. Don't let me down, but more importantly, don't let them down."

I sprinted out to the right side of the pitch, giving my teammate a high five as he came off. I got the ball to my feet almost immediately after coming on. I flew past one defender and delivered a cross into the box. Our center forward struck the ball off of the crossbar. He looked over at me and gave me a thumbs up. I continued to take players on and dispatch the ball to my teammates. I was having lots of success on the dribble. The overgrown grass might as well have been the concrete courtyards I used to play on in France. It felt the exact same to me. I was dancing around the pitch, drifting from side to side. The defenders were many times stronger than me, but it wasn't anything I wasn't used to. In my eyes, they were my cousins, or my friends. They were mirrored reflections of my brothers back home. For the first time in my life, I felt relied on. I felt as if I could positively affect my team in a way that was unique to my own individual talents. Such a responsibility instigated a feeling of ecstasy.

With 5 minutes remaining, the match remained scoreless. I received the ball just inside the opponents' half. I began to take on the opposition defenders. First one, then two, then three. I felt more and more confidence with every single player that I glided by. None of them were going to stop me. I eventually found myself in the box, just me and the goalkeeper. The entire world slowed down, and I calmly placed the ball in the bottom left corner. I wheeled away in celebration. My teammates jumped onto my back. My whole body went numb. I smiled and looked to the sky. Maybe Raphael could see me. Maybe my parents could see me. I gave the San Diego sun a cheeky wink and ran back to my own half.

Soon enough, the full time whistle blew. Stuart gave a team talk in direct reference to the one he had given less than 24 hours previously.

"All it takes is one piece of bloody magic. One piece of magic won you the match today."

I felt like the man of the moment on the ride back to the hotel. It is truly mad how one precise moment can alter an entire timeline of events.

The vibe was entirely different to yesterday's when I entered my hotel room. I collapsed onto my bed in bliss and fell asleep to the thought of what might manifest itself if I manage to produce a similar performance tomorrow against the Sounders under 23 team.

As I took the field the next evening against the Sounders, I looked back up to the sky. The sun had disappeared from view and the moon was peacefully looking down on me.

Individually, I performed well against the Sounders. I was dribbling past players with ease and working hard to track back and defend. Despite our efforts and my fairly good performance, we were losing 3-0 with 10 minutes remaining.

I managed to receive the ball just outside the box. I felt like French-Algerian superstar Riyad Mahrez as I cut in onto my left foot and curled the ball past the outstretched goalkeeper into the top corner. It was nothing more than a consolation goal, but I was hoping that it might be just enough to impress the Sounders coach into giving me a chance.

The match ended 3-1. I thanked the referees and meandered off the pitch, proud of the work I had done in the last two games in San Diego. Stuart gave me a pat on the back as I walked off.

"Great work out there, son. After we review as a team, stick around for a minute. I want to have a chat with you." He said in a reflective tone.

I tuned out during the team talk, anxious to find out what it was that Coach was going to tell me. I let everyone thank Stuart, waiting patiently to hear what he had to say.

"Lad, I had a word with the Sounders coach. He was very impressed with how you performed today and wants to have you in for a trial next week. Have a safe flight home, and their coaching staff should be in touch with you shortly."

I gave Stuart a hug and thanked him for showing unwavering faith in me since I had come to the United States. He reciprocated the positive energy and gave me his best wishes for my upcoming trial. I knew better than to be fazed at the thought of a professional trial. This was the level that I was meant to operate on now. This was the world that I was meant to dive into. I was ready for whatever existence had to throw at me. Whatever it could possibly be - if I could encounter it, it did not matter in the slightest. Despite the cognitive torture that such a notion has the capability of inducing, it sets me free. It unlocks the theoretical handcuffs that keep me from reaching for the stars.

Two weeks later, I was preparing to sign my first professional contract with the Seattle Sounders. I called my grandfather as they gathered the documents for me to print my infamous name on. I had chosen not to tell him about the trial. I used the possibility of this phone call as motivation. To know that I would be able to pick up the phone and tell my grandfather that I was a professional footballer? I couldn't picture anything better than that. When I felt myself running out of steam on the pitch, this very phone call gave me the push I needed. I punched in his digits. I never could have imagined I would be able to make this call less than a year into my stay in the United States. It was about to be the best moment of my life. This was our dream. The phone rang three times before he picked up.

"Salam Zizou, how are you? I just had dinner," I replied, acting as if nothing of particular interest was going on.

"Salam *Djiddou*. Not much is going on today," he gave a fairly mundane response.

"Nice, nice," there was a slight pause as I began to break the news to him, "actually, there is one interesting thing happening today *Inch-Allah*."

I couldn't help but begin to laugh as I said those words. He laughed back, even without knowing what it was he was about to be told. I looked out over the expansive Starfire Sports Complex. I closed my eyes and smiled. I knew that I could never forget this moment.

"What's happening today?" He cluelessly said in his raspy voice.

"It's a two year deal. I am signing a professional contract with the Seattle Sounders today *Djiddouh*. I had a trial with their under-23 team and they liked the way I played."

I could hear him begin to cry. I could see my apartment back in Barbés. I could see the mint tea glass sitting on the table. I could see my grandfather's giant eyes water up.

"I'm very proud of you Zizou. Congratulations. TabarakAllah."

His words could only express a fraction of what he was feeling. I know my grandfather. This was his dream as much as it was mine. He deserves this far more than I do. In Algerian culture, the most important part of one's character is seen in how they treat their father, and even more critically, their mother. Such an aspect of our tradition has never applied to me due to what my parents did. Because of this, all of my respect goes to my grandfather. I do this all for him. In my opinion, it's a flawed paradigm. However, it is all I have known, and all I want to do is make him proud. I responded to his heartfelt words.

"Thank you, grandfather. I will send you pictures."

As I entered the chilly room, my contract was already on the table. Before I could have a seat, I was asked what name I would like on the back of my jersey. It is customary for soccer players to put their last name on their kit, however some players put their first name or a nickname. I wasn't sure if it was wise to put my notorious last name on the kit. Just as I was about to tell the kit manager to embroider 'Zizou' onto my kit, Sofiane's words rang in my ears. He told me to never forget my identity. He told me to redefine my name. I pulled out my wallet and took a glance at the photograph of him and my father that he gave me in his kitchen on the day that I came to the United States. I knew what I had to do. I looked over to the kit manager and dramatically said my surname.

"Zenoud. Put Zenoud on the kit".

I confidently printed "Zinedine Zenoud" on the contract. I told myself that it would only be the first of many to come.

On the drive home, I asked Zakaria to play 'Love & Liberte' by Mediterranean band Gipsy Kings. My grandfather always used to play it back in Barbés. There are no words - only a wonderfully soothing Spanish guitar. I closed my eyes. It wasn't extremely blissful, but it wasn't torturous. It was expressionless. It was a state right in between pure affliction and pure ecstasy.

Chapter 10: Autre Monde: September 13. 2020

Outside of football, not much has changed in the last year and a half. Soon after I signed my contract, I rented my own apartment at Delson, a few doors down from Zakaria and his family. I paid him compensation for the year of sleeping at his place. He wouldn't accept the money at first, but I made sure he took it.

I live a fairly isolated life. I like to keep to myself. My teammates and I have a working relationship, but it isn't much more than that. Sometimes I am out at the grocery store and someone recognizes me as a Sounders player. I would be lying if I said I didn't like the attention. It gives me an amazing, albeit false sense of security that reality is indeed relevant.

I have become very close with the Wilson's in the last year or so. They live fairly close to the Sounders training center, so I often stop by and have dinner or just catch up. I have relied on Lauren a lot since I signed professionally. She's given me some really important guidance in my life, and I will forever be grateful for how she has been there for me. I've begun to open up a lot about my nihilistic thoughts to her, which is something that I never really thought I would be able to do. She obviously hasn't offered any solution, but she has been there to support me when I have needed it most. Having that number in my phone that I know I can call and safely open up to is critical to my success in all facets of my life. It gives me a safety net. I rely on the instinct that gives undisputed value to deep human connection.

On the pitch, I have been gradually climbing the ranks. Once I had assimilated into the system of the club, I was promoted to the Sounders B team. After some good performances for the B team, I was given my first training with the first team in the summer. I made my debut at the jaw-dropping CenturyLink Field in downtown Seattle about a month ago.

When my name was called by the announcer, I immediately thought home to Barbés. I knew my family and friends were all at Sofiane's, just as they said they would be. I knew they had worked all evening to configure the proper cords and find the proper illegal website to stream Major League Soccer matches. I knew they were all awake, even though it was the middle of the night, so that they could watch me take my first steps onto the pitch and hear the dozens of thousands of fans cheer me on.

For the first few minutes following my entrance in the 60th minute, I simply scanned the stadium in awe. I couldn't believe that three years ago on that day, I was in a prison cell. I couldn't believe how far I had come.

I played an average match. No goals or assists, but a fair performance for a 19-year-old on his professional debut. The kit number 93 was pinned to my back, meant to represent the scandalous area code of my birthplace in France.

Last week in training, our starting right winger sprained his ankle. I have been told I will be given a chance in our away match in Texas tonight. It was my first time traveling with the first team. It feels almost bizarre to live the life that I find myself living. One night I'm sitting in my peaceful apartment in the eastern suburbs of Seattle, and the next I'm in a tunnel halfway across the country preparing to kick a ball around in front of thousands of people.

It was a beautiful fall evening in Frisco. The temperature was perfect. The grass was perfect. The home supporters occupied the imperial red seats at the Toyota Stadium. I couldn't wait for the referee to blow the whistle and commence the match.

It was a fairly fast paced match. Both teams were playing at a high level, as you would expect. Twenty-five minutes into the match, our central defender leapt up from a corner kick and headed the ball past the FC Dallas goalkeeper. We were 1-0 up in Texas.

Just before the halftime whistle, FC Dallas were awarded a penalty. Their forward stepped up and ripped it into the right side of the goal. The match was equal once again.

I got some water and fazed out my manager's team talk. I hadn't been able to make the impact that I knew I could make. I thought back to my grandfather watching at home. I poured a bottle on my head, looked to the orange sky and ran out for the second half.

I received the ball soon after the start of the second half and was stripped of possession by a wonderful tackle from the FC Dallas full back. Our center forward yelled out to me.

"Kid, pass the ball! You are only on the pitch because of an injury".

I had to prove him wrong. I played simple for the next few minutes before once again attempting to make a difference.

With twenty minutes remaining, I heard chanting coming from visibly drunk fans on my side of the pitch. They began to make racist remarks towards me and started to reference the attacks. I didn't believe it was real. It felt like I was in a nightmare. The fans were escorted out of the stadium within the blink of an eye. I got the ball to my feet far inside the opposing teams half. After playing a one-two combination with the same central forward who had criticized me a half an hour before, I blasted the ball towards the goal. It struck the post and hit the back of the Dallas net. I immediately sprinted over to the section of red seats where the fans had been shouting at me and cupped my ears signaling that I couldn't hear them. The more civilized Dallas fans gave me a standing ovation in recognition of the discrimination I had just received.

When the full whistle was blown, I once again looked up to the sky. I once again wondered if Raphael could see me. I once again wondered if my parents could see me. I gave another wink, just as I had done in San Diego almost two years previously.

The weeks continued to fly by, and I continued to run around in the circles that modern society offered me. Winning goals against Atlanta United, San Jose Earthquakes and Orlando City came in the months following my heroics in Texas. I was beginning to make a name for myself.

I'm not afraid to say that I am absolutely inclined towards losing myself in my new-found money and fame. As I previously stated, the attention fabricates a rush in my veins. I am incapable of dreading existence when a stadium full of supporters is chanting my name. Materialistic goods provide enough of a materialistic allure for me to subconsciously accept a form of materialism. That's my nature. I count my lucky stars that I am able to keep myself occupied by my irrelevant blessings found in this life.

I send money and gifts back to Barbés as often as I can. I even offered to move my grandfather to a nicer part of town, but he refused profusely. He insisted that he would never leave Barbés. It is his community. He told me he would rather live in Barbés than on the Champs-Élysées, despite the fact that our district was one of the most crime-ridden neighborhoods in Western Europe. He knew everyone, everyone knew him. They would always be there for each other. I couldn't blame him for his reliance and loyalty to those who he considered family. I find that part of his personality extremely admirable.

Wissam ended up becoming a butcher, and Mamadou is employed at a coffee shop. A few days ago, Mamadou told me that Ibrahim had just dropped out of university and was getting involved with some sketchy individuals who had recently been released from prison. I asked Wissam if Mamadou was telling the truth, and he told me that he hadn't spoken to Ibrahim in almost six months. I have a trip scheduled to Paris at the beginning of January, which is in three weeks. It will be my first time returning home since coming to the United States. I intend to get the crew back together, but I am incredibly worried about Ibrahim and his well-being. It sounds as if he is searching for his lost identity in the banlieue - which almost always results in prison, radicalization or both.

I had extremely mixed emotions about returning to Paris. On one hand, I was going to return a hero. I made it out. I had become a role model for many of the kids in Barbés. On the other hand, I wasn't sure if I was ready to confront the demons I had left behind in France.

Zakaria was working on the day of my flight, so Lauren had offered to drive me to the airport. My mind was jumping from place to place as we sped down the highway in her unexpectedly giant Ford truck. It didn't take long before she noticed something was up.

"What's going on Zinedine?"

I replied, putting my thoughts into words the best I could. I could sense the shakiness in my voice. Lauren is the only person I will open up to, but I still struggle to get everything out.

"Lauren, I just don't know what to expect. I have a feeling that returning to France will break me from this trance-like state that I've become accustomed to in the United States. I left so much back in Barbés. I hope I haven't changed much from when I left. I just don't know if I became the person I was meant to become, you know?"

Lauren gave me a response that put me at ease, at least for the time being, "You can't repeat the past. You can't ponder roads not taken. Every struggle, every action, and every thought has made you the person you are today. Everything that happens today determines who you will be tomorrow. You have to enjoy the little things in life. You'll be ok kid. Just smile and enjoy your time at home. Maybe you'll learn a little more about yourself."

When we pulled up to the gate, she unlocked the door, looked at me with her intense eyes and gave me the emotional security I needed.

"Call me at any time if you ever need anything. Don't do anything stupid or I will find out about it. Take pictures. See you soon Zinedine."

I expressed a laugh and gave a wave before wandering into the ever-crowded Sea-Tac airport. The feeling around the airport was much different nowadays than when I first arrived almost two years previously.

I had been listening to the soul-numbingly dark musical creations of The Weeknd ever since the brokenhearted man named Anthony had played one of his tracks for me on my plane ride to the United States. I wondered where he was now as I listened to "Rolling Stone" a track off Tesfaye's mixtape "Thursday."

Tp, cbcz, mpwf nf, pi
Cfgpsf uifz bmm mpwf nf
Voujm zpv xpo'u mpwf nf, pi
Cfdbvtf uifz'mm bmm mpwf nf, ppi
J'mm cf ejggfsfou, pi
J uijol J'mm cf ejggfsfou, ppi
J ipqf J'n opu ejggfsfou, pi
Boe J ipqf zpv'mm tujmm mjtufo

The Weeknd knew he would be famous. Even when he was homeless, he knew he would take the music industry by storm. That was his destiny. It had to happen. He knew the world would love him. He knew that he would acclimate himself to fame in order to more adequately cope with his sorrow. He knew he had to be different. But part of him - the humanity in his disillusioned soul - didn't want to leave his demons behind. He felt pity for the pain that had plagued him for so long. He felt as if part of his identity was being ripped from him, and for better or for worse, that left him with intense emotion.

Was it true? Only he knew. But such a sentiment did occupy my thoughts for a good portion of the flight. I tried not to think about things too much. I watched a whole season of Parks N' Rec, one of the old Iron Man movies, and of course - a soccer match. It was Algeria's first World Cup match ever - an iconic date with West Germany in June 1982. Despite the some 38 years that have passed since the match had been played, the Algerian people would never forget upsetting all odds and beating the world-class West German side 2-1, becoming the first ever African side to beat a European team at a World Cup.

Algeria went on to lose to Austria and beat Chile. Ordinarily, two wins would be enough for a team to advance out of their group into the second round. However, Germany and Austria fixed their match - in what would later be called 'The Disgrace of Gijon' meaning that the two European sides would advance at the expense of the Algerian team. We would have to wait 34 years to win a match at a World Cup - a 4-2 demolition of South Korea in the 2014 edition of the tournament. That emphatic win gave

Algeria the confidence to draw 1-1 with Russia, meaning that we would advance to the second round of the World Cup for the first time in our history. Our opponents? Germany.

I tuned into the match from Barbés with my grandfather. He often recalled the disappointment of 1982, citing that there would never be an Algerian team like the one from the '80's.

"Madjer and Belloumi, those guys were legends. They deserved to lead the team into the last 16," he often said when I asked about the team.

He was right about that. Rabah Madjer scored a stunning backheel winning goal in the 1987 UEFA Champions League Final, the most important match of the calendar year for football fans. Lakhdar Belloumi is credited with inventing the widely popular "blind pass". They each scored goals against West Germany - goals that would go down in Algerian folklore.

"The most important thing was that they played with passion. They were born in Algeria. They were born at a time when the French were massacring our citizens and we were fighting for our independence. When they stepped out on the field, it was about more than football. They were representing every Algerian citizen. They were fighting to protect the flag that millions died for," my grandfather said when comparing the current team to the players of his era to the players of my era.

He was arguably right about that too. In his day, everyone on the Algeria national team wanted to be there. Nowadays, there are certainly passionate players - but there are undoubtedly those who are only there because they didn't end up good enough to play for France. After all, most of the national side was born in France, and most of the truly exciting French born Algerian prospects have decided to represent the French team. It isn't that they don't love Algeria, or that they don't understand the history. It seems as if the past that fueled the golden generation of the 80's was no longer lingering on the minds of the players, with the heartbreak and subsequent desire confined to the history books.

Despite the criticism of the modern national side, they did become the first Algerian team to ever reach the second round of the World Cup in 2014. We didn't beat Germany in the Round of 16, but we took them farther than any other team did for the remainder of the tournament, as the Germans went on to become world champions. The world was proud of our performance, and even the Germans gave us their respect.

Algerian football has come leaps and bounds in the last 10 years. Riyad Mahrez was a thin, inconsistent 23-year-old when he was surprisingly called up to play in the 2014 World Cup. Only 2 years later, he had been the best player in a Leicester City team that had provided arguably the biggest upset in sporting history when they won the English Premier League title against all odds. A few days before I got out of jail, he became the most expensive African player of all time when Manchester City paid over 60 million pounds to lure him away from Leicester City. He is quite possibly the best player that Algeria has ever had, but with his often dyed hair and high pitched French accent, he is definitely a far-cry from the industrious, Algerian born players of the 80's.

Regardless, he is still a huge inspiration of mine. In 2009, if you told 18-year-old Mahrez, a player who was struggling to perform in the French amateur divisions, that within 5 years he would be at a World Cup, and that within 7 years he would win BBC's award for the best African player in the world, he would probably laugh and ask to take a hit of whatever you were smoking. Even with his struggles, such as the passing of his father when he was 15, he managed to make it to the top. I reckon it takes a lot of mental strength to do that.

Before he passed, a young Mahrez assured his father that he would win the African Cup for the Algerian national team one day. When I first moved to America, it seemed incredibly unlikely he would ever be able to fulfill that promise. Algeria had been miserable at the African Cup of Nations in almost every edition since they had won the tournament on home soil in 1990. I watched with my disappointed grandfather as the supposed 'golden generation' failed to perform in the 2015 and 2017 tournaments respectively. After burning through a treacherous 5 coaches in 2 years and finishing bottom of their 2018 World Cup qualifying group, an injury plagued Algeria were once again expected to flop at the 2019 African Cup.

However, Algeria were extremely impressive in the group stages of the tournament. The Desert Foxes did not concede a goal, and even beat tournament favorites Senegal thanks to a sublime strike by Mohamed Youcef Belaili - a player with tremendous amounts of unfulfilled talent who had been banned from football for 2 years in 2015 after a positive cocaine test. This team was filled with outcasts, rejects, and underdogs.

Zakaria, Zahia, Ilyas and I continued to watch Algeria gain momentum. As tournament hosts and bitter rivals Egypt fell to South Africa in the first knockout, Algeria disposed of Guinea. Riyad Mahrez killed the game off in the second half with a deft touch and brilliant finish, but Belaili once again was the player to open the scoring - playing a delightful one-two with his childhood friend and academy teammate Baghad Bounedjah. We then went on to beat Ivory Coast in a nervy penalty shootout that left the entire Algeria squad and staff with tears of joy when the final whistle blew. This generation was finally showing the desire they lacked. It seemed as if no one was going to beat *Les Fennecs*. It seemed as if they were finally going to go all the way. The manager was Djamel Belmadi - a 43-year-old Parisian born Algerian who had captained Algeria in the 2004 African Cup. The young coach was orchestrating a historic journey. I FaceTimed my grandfather during the penalty shootout. We shouted, screamed, laughed and smiled in unison from across the world. Algeria were to play Nigeria in the semifinals of the African Cup. If they were to win, they would compete in their first cup final in 29 years.

The match was a scrappy 1-1 affair which had seen goals scored from an own goal and penalty for each side respectively. The game seemed destined for extra time. In the final few seconds, Arsenal reject Ismael Bennacer won a free kick on the edge of the Nigerian box. Riyad Mahrez calmly stepped up to take the final shot of the match. The dark Cairo sky provided a backdrop for the astronomical possibilities of the ensuing strike. Legendary

Algerian commentator Hafid Derradji could be heard through millions of TV screens across the globe repeatedly shouting, "Put it in the goal Riyad, put it in the goal Riyad!"

Mahrez followed Derradji's order. The 28-year-old powered the ball into the top left corner with the final touch of the match. Derradji began crying as he announced the goal, and as Mahrez ran the length of the pitch celebrating. Zakaria and I ran out into the usually quiet halls of Delson Apartments and celebrated like all of our sorrow had been washed away. Football can do that to you.

A second date with Senegal was set for July 19, 2019. I had read during the week on Twitter that it seemed "written in the stars" for this Algeria team to win this African Cup of Nations. The passion was off the charts.

Fate seemed to dictate the final more than any player performance or tactical decision. The jam-packed International Stadium of Cairo was sent into absolute shock as Baghdad Bounedjah scored the opening goal seconds into the game. It wasn't pretty - the shot took possibly the most wicked deflection that I have ever seen, and eventually looped over the standstill Senegalese keeper. Bounedjah didn't care how it went in. Zakaria and I watching didn't care how it went in. Derradji, who was once again going wild over the microphone, certainly did not care how it went in. It was in. We jumped off the couch and ran around my cramped apartment.

The shot was to be Algeria's only shot on target for the entire 94 minutes. It was Senegal attack after Senegal attack for the remainder of the match, but the rock-solid Algerian defense stood strong. Baghdad Bounedjah scored the goal that was to go down in history as the one that brought the African Cup back to Algeria. The final whistle blew. Algeria were African Champions for the first time in 29 years. I called my grandfather and could hear him fighting back tears.

"The young ones finally did it. They finally brought the trophy back home. Enjoy this moment, Zizou."

I certainly was. I had always seen myself playing for France if I was given the opportunity - but watching those Algerian players celebrate was something else. Watching a team that consisted of individuals so similar to myself finally live the moment they had been waiting for their whole lives. It really made me ask questions about my identity. French-Algerian? Algerian-French? Maybe I wasn't fully Algerian and maybe I wasn't fully French, but I was certainly leaning towards my heritage.

Matters in France didn't help. Conflicts between Algerian supporters and police resulted in dozens of injuries and hundreds of arrests during the celebrations. The far-right was painting the image of the "uncivilized, invader, Arab football fan", despite the fact that the French public were doing the exact same when they had won the World Cup only twelve months previous. It had been over a year and a half since our exploits in the African Cup. I was reminded of the adventure because of the track faintly playing in my popping ears as the airplane descended towards *Paname*. "Tahia" was a tune released by PNL only minutes after we captured the trophy. A melodic guitar is the base for the catchy beat.

Tahia, Tahia, PNL
Tahia, Tahia, Djazair
Tahia, Tahia, PNL
Tahia, Tahia, Djazair

When I got off the airplane, the ashy Parisian air filled my conflicted lungs. A psychotic intuition directed my actions, leaving me disconnected from reality as I made my way through the airport. I felt as if every dark moment from my past had been erased. I felt as if all the sins I had committed were in a different dimension. Everything I pondered continued to confuse my inquisitive mind.

The hug my grandfather gave me when he picked me up from the airport could not be done justice by my writing ability. Once he let go, he looked me dead in the eyes and failed to hold in tears of joy. Last time he had seen me, I had just gotten out of prison. Now I was an established professional footballer. I don't really know how it happened. Some combination of hard work, willpower and lots of luck.

I was overcome with a strong, undistinguished emotion. I put my shaky left hand on the ever cold, stained gold doorknob to my childhood home. The feeling was stronger than even those I felt when I returned from prison. It was the type of feeling that allows you to find some hope in your future. For as long as I can remember, fate has been the antagonist. Fate had decided that I was the enemy. Fate had sent me to jail. Fate had created every bit of anger that I redirected towards it. Nowadays? Fate was my friend. Fate ripped apart my dreams and wrote new ones for me.

My grandfather and I didn't have much to catch up on as we already spoke on video chat every single day.

Although my career was yet to be extremely lucrative, I had made a fair amount of money. Additionally, I recently signed an endorsement deal with PUMA which sees me earn a pretty penny for promoting their products. All in all, my income was much higher than I would've expected to be earning at the age of 19. I knew from the start that my first bit of profit would go towards my grandfather. After hours of haggling, I eventually convinced him to accept the 20,000 Euro check that I had written him. It would be the first of many.

After an afternoon nap, I decided to take a stroll to Sofiane's. Nostalgic emotions were kicking in but more so a sensation of dissociation. I felt so disconnected from my timeline. Nothing felt real at all. I zoned out, unable to focus on forming any coherent thoughts and unable to focus on my surroundings. I felt as if I was acting out my story and not living it. Something felt wrong inside my head. I couldn't tell if I was dreaming or awake. The border between reality and illusion entirely blurred and for some reason, I was alright with that.

I had arranged for Wissam to meet me at Sofiane's. A bell jangled as I pushed open the door of the restaurant.

"Ah, look who it is!" Sofiane ran over and gave me a comforting hug.

After greeting Sofiane, I turned the corner to the main seating area to find Wissam at the table we always sit at. He got up and gave me a hug. He had grown since the last time I saw him. Not only was he taller, but he was carrying some baggage. You could see it in his eyes.

Wissam and I chatted about everything - football, Paris, Seattle, my Grandfather, music. Eventually, I shifted the conversation into the direction he knew it was headed.

"So, you really haven't talked to Ibrahim in 6 months?"

He fidgeted with his utensils and attempted to respond to my inquiry with as much conviction as possible.

"Yeah. He just seemed to fall off the map. He dropped out of university and disappeared. He won't answer my calls or texts."

Something was wrong. I could feel it. Before Wissam even finished talking, I started punching in Ibrahim's digits on my phone. It rang twice before he picked up. He formally greeted me in Arabic. His voice was much more drained than the last time I heard it.

"*Salam U Alaikum Wa Rahmatullah Wa Barakatuh,*" he said.

"Ibrahim, where are you? I'm home. I want to see you." I replied.

His tone entirely changed, "Zizou?"

He cleared his throat and spoke with the drained voice once again.

"I'm in Drancy. Come meet me here. I will send you my location. No one else, just you."

"I'll swing by within the next hour. See you inch-Allah. Salam," I wanted to see him as soon as possible.

He hung up the phone without a response. By now, Sofiane had sat down near us. Wissam quickly explained to him the situation while I was on the phone. I caught them both up.

"He wants me to meet him in Drancy. Alone."

Sofiane looked very concerned. He took off his vivid orange bandana and held it in his greasy hands. The air was the same as it had always been. The floors were stained just how they always had been. The food tasted just like it always had.

"I'll go with you."

Sofiane and I cleaned up the restaurant a bit before heading to the metro. He gave my grandfather a call and told him that we were going to meet Ibrahim and that we would be home soon.

"So, how's my brother?" He asked as I sat on the metro.

Just as the elements of Sofiane's restaurant, the metro was also the same as it always had been. Inquisitive stares of curious civilians who know my demeanor is different in comparison to the rest of the population. We all like to think we are unique, but I know I am. I have always known I am. That isn't meant to sound arrogant or pretentious. It is just the way things are. It doesn't matter, but it is indeed the way things are.

"Zinedine?" Sofiane nudged me on the shoulder; I had zoned out.

"He's doing good. I really have loved getting to know him."

We got off the metro and made our way to the address that Ibrahim sent to us. It was a rundown building across the street from some housing projects. It appeared to be an old cafe, but any markings were unclear.

"I'll just be outside. Call me if you need anything," Sofiane said as he pulled out his dab pen and took a hit, blowing the smoke in the opposite direction of myself.

I knocked on the scratched door. After a few seconds, Ibrahim came and creaked it open. I could barely see inside. The lighting was dim and the environment was hard to recognize. Once he saw it was me, he fully opened the door and invited me inside. No smile. No hug.

Upon entry, I was greeted with the intense smell of cannabis, something I have become familiar with in Seattle. Dirty dishes and wrinkled papers covered every inch of the black granite countertop. A messy, round table was unoccupied. Ibrahim signaled for me to take a seat.

I sat down at the table with my old friend. He was wearing a giant leather jacket and faded, loose, blue jeans. He had a crazed look in his eyes.

"How is America?" He asked me.

The question seemed slightly out of place. I had just followed all of his sketchy instructions to find myself in his sketchy apartment, and he provides zero context.

"It's good. How's France? Is this your new place?" I replied.

He pulled out an e-cigarette and took a hit, blowing the smoke into the already hazy air. He coughed mercilessly and then responded.

"Yeah, but I have a roommate."

He provided no more details than that. Following this, there was a short pause. Ibrahim took a few more hits and hacked out a few more unpleasant coughs. My psychology wouldn't allow me to just let this one go. Something was severely wrong, and I had to figure it out. I had my suspicions, and unfortunately, I was about to be proven right.

"Do you ever wonder why we make the choices we make Zizou? Do you believe you have full control over your decisions, or are you just playing your part in fate? Are you just simply running in circles, feeling emotions you were always meant to feel? Emotions that you were predisposed to experiencing. Sensations that you have absolutely no power over."

It was an unprecedented shift of focus. He posed an interesting question, but not one that I was expecting to find myself reflecting on at this point in time. I didn't open my mouth and reply. After a short pause, he continued in what came across like a flowing freestyle of feelings disguised as philosophical thoughts.

"I mean, why do anything at all? Why feel anything at all? It all seems so methodical and mundane. Our society solely exists and functions properly because of tendencies that we as humans cannot avoid. What's to stop me from going against that?"

His words induced anxiety in my nostalgic soul. As he concluded his sentence, he leaned down towards the floor and grabbed something heavy and metal from the dusty floor. I could see his arms shake as he held the AR-15 rifle in his ashy hands. His limbs, eyes, and soul shook to an uncontrollable degree. I jumped out of my seat.

"What the hell Ibrahim? Are you insane?" I exclaimed.

"Hold it," he whispered.

He dropped the rifle in my general direction. I instinctively grabbed it, not letting it crash onto the dirty hardwood floor.

"Don't you feel something stirring inside? Don't you feel like you now wield a power that they never wanted you to wield?"

My vision blurred as I refused to accept that he was right. The lizard part of my brain felt pure pleasure at the control I so naturally commanded. As soon as I got comfortable holding the rifle, I looked up at Ibrahim. He was still shuffling back and forth, clearly uncomfortable with his newfound purpose. For a split second, I saw my father. So vulnerable. So lost. I closed my eyes immediately and saw Nathan Wilson's image fly across my mind. I halfheartedly looked down at the rifle, feeling as if I was about to faint. A shockwave of pain penetrated my arms, and I dropped the weapon. It crashed onto the hardwood floor. I looked over at Ibrahim and finally replied.

"Our thirst for power comes from the same unconscious part of our minds that shaped our destinies. Our enlightenment is built on the same principles of our discrimination. At the end of the day, we have no control other than what our perspective allows us to control."

At the conclusion of my sentence, Ibrahim began to cry, "I don't know what I want. I feel myself running in circles. I feel myself searching for happiness in all the wrong places."

My eyes jumped between Ibrahim's expression of discomfort and the assault rifle on the floor. A distorted police siren was drained out by the tears of my friend. I gave him a hug. I can't put it in any more eloquent language than that. The room was void of purity. It felt heartless and ironically cold. The manifestation of our countless sins.

"Let's go back to Sofiane's," I quietly told him as he began to come down from his peak of despair.

Ibrahim and I moseyed out to Sofiane. Once they had exchanged pleasantries, we all took the metro back home. I left Ibrahim in the restaurant with Sofiane to talk about his issues. I trusted Sofiane more than anyone to calm my friend down and snap him back into reality. After all, this has all happened before. I walked home through the blackness of the banlieue. I let myself lose my mind in the moment. The air was polluted with the smell of cigarette smoke, the eerie feeling of regret, and full of suppressed fear. As I walked, I looked around and attempted to recollect all of the childhood memories I had along these streets. I smiled as I remembered every Eid, birthday, and moment of lucidity. I wish I could do it all over again, not to change anything, but to experience that innocent perspective once again. The eerie and reflective production of "Dangerous" by SchoolboyQ and Kid Cudi was playing in my headphones.

J'n gffmjoh ebohfspvt, J'n gffmjoh obvtfpvt
Spbe mfgu nf dsbaz, tpbsjoh, J xboob

Hsffu nf cz nz iboe 'ujm zpv ufbdi nf up gmpbu
Ifbe jt jo uif dmpve xjui nz tupnbdi cmpx
Tpnfuijo' 'cpvu uijt gffmjoh, J gfmu ju cfgpsf

Qjodi nf po nz bsn, jt ju Ifbwfo ps gvo?

Jg J epo'u dpnf cbdl, ibe b ifmm pg b svo

Ipx nboz gsjfoet bspvoe nf ifmqjoh nf mptf?

Ipx nboz fydvtft voujm J'n fydvtfe?

Tibepx nz npsojoh, J bjo'u esfbnjoh ju sjhiu

Bjo'u op xbz b gmpxfs dpvme cmppn jo uif ojhiu

Gbnjmz usjfe up xbso nf, dpvmeo'u lffq nf bxbz

'Ujm J gjhvsf gmzjoh, J cfuufs ftdbqf

I wanted those memories to matter. I wanted my nostalgia to be the backstory for my eventual legacy. I relied on the possible grandiosity of my future to carry me through the present.

The rest of my trip can only be defined as a blur. I spent time with my grandfather. I spent time kicking it with Wissam and Mamadou. I spent time rehabilitating Ibrahim and updating Sofiane on my journey. I spent time wandering the dark, dangerous roads that I knew as well as I knew myself. However, within the blink of an eye, I was back at Charles de Gaulle Airport. Life itself had become fuzzy. My experiences and emotions were no longer predictable. My perspective shifted every day. I felt as if I was losing a true sense of reality. My conscious mind felt as if it had shut off, leaving me clawing at thin air. Real and fake had slowly grown more and more similar, and as I boarded the airplane back to Seattle, they were practically synonymous.

Chapter 11: Dans La Ville: June 30, 2021

Upon the completion of our preseason, the team was preparing for our first competitive match of the new year - a home match against elite Mexican side Santos Laguna. Santos Laguna are one of the biggest clubs in Mexico and would be traveling to Seattle for a match in the CONCACAF Champions League. The CONCACAF Champions League is a competition with the most elite clubs on the North American continent.

The unique nature of each season in Seattle was something truly special. It wasn't difficult to witness the leaves change into warm shades of yellow, orange and red every Halloween. Every night in spring, a chorus of frogs could be heard outside my apartment window. In the morning, the birds woke me up with the tune of ancient songs. I found myself attaching memories and moments to each part of the year. Hebb's Law was constantly proving itself true in my young brain.

I spent a lot of time in downtown Seattle. The city was absolutely gorgeous. The modern Seattle skyline felt profound, important, and seductive. I often meandered aimlessly around the vibrant streets and alleyways, gauging the masses and going on adventures. I liked to wander past the Space Needle, I liked to eat at *Crepe de Paris* inside Pike Place Market when I was homesick. I liked to walk through the ghetto. I liked to sit on benches and converse with the homeless of the city. Everyone deserves to be heard. It is not my place to judge others for their sins, their past or their condition. The world has already been hard enough on them, and if I had the opportunity to offer some relief, I always did. Everyone has a unique perspective, and something can be learned from that. When I had a little extra money in my pocket, I liked to take some of the homeless into the grocery store and buy them a full shopping cart of food. I would be lying if part of it wasn't to make myself feel important and needed, and I am willing to admit that. However, I did care. I truly care about people. The world is unforgiving. Psychology is unforgiving. Existence is unforgiving.

It wasn't hard to find men and women struggling to survive on the streets of the city, no matter the time of day or day of the week. Seattle is one of the most expensive cities in the United States, and in juxtaposition to the extremely wealthy individuals in the area, there is a large homeless population. Many in the city blame the homeless themselves and the abuse of illegal substances for the situation, but I find that extremely biased and unproductive. They need help and ridiculing them for their past and pain will do nothing but increase tension and cause a lot of unnecessary existential panic. Truthfully, most people cannot afford to live in Seattle or the suburbs, even with a job. If a society cannot support such a sizable amount of the population, then that society is flawed. It breaks my heart to see the hopelessness in the eyes of the homeless, college students and even children of the city. In some ways, it almost feels apocalyptic. The rich can only get so much richer and the poor can only get so much poorer.

The Ides of March set the day for our clash with Santos Laguna. Traffic clogged the city as the daylight dwindled. I started the match in my favored position on the right flank of the field. I adjusted the sleeves of my bright green jersey as I waited for the referee to begin the match.

Thirty seconds into the match, we won a corner. Our center midfielder whipped it in, and the ball was cleared out by the other team's defense. It fell right to me at the edge of the 18 yard box. Without taking a touch, I belted the ball on frame with too much venom for the goalkeeper to handle.

By the end of the ninety minutes, the score was 3-1. I had scored all three goals. As per tradition, if a player manages to score three or more goals in a match, they are entitled to keep the ball used in the game. I collected the match ball and left the stadium with a swagger to my stride. My teammates dapped me up as I exited.

Upon my return to Delson, I opened up my phone and saw my friends from France hyping me up on Snapchat. Mamadou, Wissam and Ibrahim sent me videos of them celebrating the goals with a glass of Orangina in one hand and a napoleon in the other. It truly did put a smile on my face to see them supporting me. Just as I wrote earlier, my crew was all I had. Despite the good fortune that I find myself reaping the successes of, I will never forget their support and where I come from. My grandfather taught me that. Sofiane taught me that. The rest of this glitter and glamour is temporary. My family is everything I have.

Just as I was getting too tired to process my perspective and was about to put my phone away, I received a message from a French number on WhatsApp. It was a football agent named

Munir Doukha. He congratulated me on my performance and asked me if I was interested in joining French side Red Star Paris FC. Red Star are a historic club in Paris. At the time of the call, they were leading the French second division. It was very likely that they would get promoted and be a Ligue 1 team in the 2021-2022 season. The thought of playing in front of my grandfather was far too incredible of an opportunity for me to let slip away.

I had three years remaining on my contract at the Seattle Sounders. I renewed my deal in the fall. In the days following Munir's first text, I had discussed with representatives directly from Red Star. We swiftly agreed on personal terms regarding my contract. All that had to be sorted out was a transfer fee. Red Star told me that they were willing to pay the Seattle Sounders a maximum of two million euros for my services.

I tried to ignore the transfer talk when I stepped onto the pitch, but it was hard not to think about it. My performances in training became less impressive, and I was starting to fantasize about the future and forget about the present. The club was most certainly not pleased. They organized a meeting with me on April Fools' Day. My manager and I met at a quaint coffee shop in Capitol Hill called Puzzles.

In my time at the Sounders, three managers had come and gone. The current one was former Wolverhampton Wanderers midfielder Carl Robinson. The Welshman had previously managed our rivals Vancouver Whitecaps, and controversially joined us after the sacking of our previous coach last August. He had steadied the ship, and we had a good working relationship.

I walked into the cozy coffee shop and found my manager sitting at a wooden table near the entrance. I had been here many times, and I loved the atmosphere. There were lots of plants around the place that made the air feel fresh and natural. Carl took a sip of his latte and asked me about my desire to move to Red Star and leave Seattle. I decided that I had to be transparent and honest to the club. Not only had they given me my entire career, but I knew that I had the best chance of leaving if I simply told them why. I wasn't going to let anything stop me from making this transfer.

"I have an EU passport and I grew up in Paris. My grandfather and best friends live in the city. I speak French fluently and miss home. Additionally, Red Star will likely compete in Ligue 1 next year. The prospect of playing in one of the 'Big 5' leagues in Europe is extremely enticing."

Mr. Robinson nodded his head in agreement.

"Zinedine, I completely understand your ambition and I respect your wishes. I have played in Europe and the United States, and I can imagine your excitement at this possibility. We will let you go during Red Star's preseason, which starts July 1st. However, this is on the assumption that you will continue to give everything to Seattle Sounders until your contract is terminated. You are a critical player for us, and I need you to be focused and sharp. If I noticed continued lapses in concentration, I will call the deal off and hold you to your contract. It's all in your hands now lad," He said.

I smiled and gave him a firm handshake. I thanked him for his cooperation and promised him that I would not let him down. I meant that when I said it. I am fueled by nostalgia, and I knew that someday the Seattle Sounders and my time in Washington State would simply be a blissful memory. I wanted to end this chapter of my life and career on a positive note.

For the next few months, I pushed myself to continue working hard. My transfer had quite predictably been leaked to the press, and my friends and family were extremely excited to have me return to France. I found myself on YouTube watching American pundits attempt to predict how I would do in France. It felt so surreal to hear them say my name and read facts about my life off a piece of paper in their sports studio. Life changed so quickly. I often forgot where I was, where I was going, and how I felt back in France.

Even as I consciously make an effort to recall my angst, it seems like it was a world away. The past turmoil is clouded by the temporary blessings of today.

My teammates on the Sounders were all supportive of my move. I rarely write about it, but a lot of these guys had become my brothers. We spend so much time together, and I intend to stay in touch with them no matter where our careers progress.

Even though I could drive and had no reason to, I still found myself walking around town a lot. I liked to ride my bike down in the town of Issaquah all the way down Newport Way into the larger city of Bellevue. It was a peaceful ride. The air was always fresh and the trees were always green. It felt like nothing outside of that road existed or mattered. There were no wars going on in faraway lands. There was no political divide in America. There was not even an impending sense of doom that came with simply existing. There was no pain. All that existed was the trees around me, the road in front of me, and the music in my headphones. This evening, a whimsical, floaty composition titled "Dream Sweet in Sea Major," played in my headphones as I whizzed past cars, churches, houses and children.

A group of children
The galaxy extends
A garden of imagination
Bridging the gap
Skating past the moon
As we evolve
It feels like flying
But maybe we're dying.

At the end of my ride, I found myself near Tyee Middle School. As I took off my headphones, I heard the echo of voices singing from inside. Outside the building, I saw a sign advertising their Spring Choral Concert that was set to take place that night. I meandered inside the theater holding my Mexican Coca-Cola and took a seat. I didn't really make a conscious decision to go watch the performance. It felt as if I was on my bike one minute and watching the vocal performance the next. I had completely dissociated. Despite the picturesque clear conditions of the Seattle sky, my memory and concentration were very hazy.

The youthful voices of the performers ignited a missing piece from my own childhood. It was hard for me to watch the kids' parents look on and wave at their children with faces full of unconditional love. It was excruciating. I tried to picture my parents in that crowd, giving smiles and clapping at the show of music and growth. I couldn't imagine it in the slightest. That sense of abandonment leaves me feeling lost in existence. I wander around searching for a purpose that was broken years ago, on a timeline I can't even begin to understand. I felt my eyes water as I blinked rapidly. I couldn't stop my eyelids from repeatedly opening and closing.

As my heart raced, the children were finishing their concert. The final song was "Bohemian Rhapsody" by the legendary band Queen. I was struggling to pay attention, but they were doing an incredible job. By the end of the piece, a young boy came up to the microphone and stood confidently on the stage. His suit and tie were clearly too large for him, but he did not care. He looked out at the audience and sang the final words of the song with a scratchiness and softness to his juvenile voice.

> Opuijoh sfbmmz nbuufst,
> Bozpof dbo tff.
> Opuijoh sfbmmz nbuufst
> Opuijoh sfbmmz nbuufst up nf.

I fell into a state of panic as the audience cheered. I immediately made my way to the exit door. I made the profound realizations that I had spent my entire existence running from. Severely angered at my inability to sync up with reality, I threw my coke bottle onto Newport Way. The glass shattered into a million pieces all across the bumpy road. The air felt as if it was pulling me towards doom. I got on my bike and pedaled as fast as I could in no particular direction. I went up a steep hill and found myself in a lavish neighborhood. I started to slow down my bike as I looked to the sky and counted the distant stars.

As I got to the top of the hill, I turned my head and looked over the trees I just rode past. It was the most gorgeous view I had ever laid my eyes on. Downtown Seattle, Bellevue, the lakes, bridges and greenery could all be seen. The city was full of sinful influence, but the sky was the same it had been thousands of years ago. I got off my bike and sat atop the hill, the music in my ears tying itself to the memory. It was a bittersweet moment, stained with a blissful ignorance. I felt myself counting my blessings right alongside my misfortune. I felt utterly disoriented at my place in everything. It wasn't meant to be philosophical or spiritual, but more so a rational realization of the unreliable patternicity that makes everything seem normal.

I headed home and felt myself close my mind. I forced myself to reassimilate into my reality. I felt so hopelessly trapped in the human condition. I felt a strong, viscous and continuous cycle of irony and anger directed towards my own human desires, emotions, tendencies and thoughts. I felt lost in a world that provided no guarantees of closure. I felt myself spiraling into the habit of understanding the world through a certain paradigm. I once read that the only way one can think critically about any given concept is to acknowledge the fact that they inherently have a tremendous amount of bias and an immeasurably filtered view of reality, the universe and everything within comprehension. The frustration that is caused by the fact that such frustration is in and of itself an aspect of this filtered reality is a thought loop that will forever push me into an extremely dissociative state.

My performances in my last few months in Seattle were fairly mundane. I didn't put my best numbers forward, but no one at the club truly pinned blame on me. The manager believed that I was working as hard as I could and that I was just not firing on all cylinders. My final match was on June 26, 2021 at home against our bitter rivals Portland Timbers. I was preparing myself for the perfect send off. Before the match, I printed a T-shirt with a farewell message for the Sounders supporters. I wore it under my rave green Seattle jersey, and visualized myself ripping off my #93 kit and throwing it into the crowd.

The match was deadlocked at 0-0 for over 75 minutes. Both teams had hit the woodwork in the first half. The commentators repeated that it would take a piece of magic to separate the two sides.

I received the ball near the halfway line and played a firm pass towards my teammate just outside the box. He took a touch and prepared to have a strike. However, just as he was about to blast the ball, the Portland defender clipped his leg. The referee blew his whistle and gave us a free kick right on the edge of the box. I stood over the ball as the referee adjusted the wall. I looked at the goalkeeper and looked down at my purple cleats. I knew that this was my perfect chance to make the fans smile one last time. I struck the ball just over the wall, and it slammed against the crossbar. The ball bounced off the crossbar onto the ground, then back out of the goal. The stadium let out a collective, ferocious roar. I looked anxiously at the referee, unsure whether the ball had crossed the line. He looked at his watch and pointed towards the center circle, indicating that the goal-line technology confirmed that the ball had crossed the line. Soon enough my teammates were piling on top of me at the corner flag. It was a moment of inspiration. It was a moment I will never forget. I tore off my jersey and displayed my undershirt to the stadium. Many of them gave me a standing ovation as they saw the shirt, which read "Thank you Seattle, I will always love you." I struggled to hold back a tear or two. All life is are the moments that can swallow you into the euphoria and spit you out refreshed and ultimately blind. That is all self-actualization could ever possibly be.

In my last few days in Seattle, I thanked my coaches, teammates and friends for everything they had done for me. Seattle would always be special to me. I got off the plane two years ago as a naive and anxious boy, and I got back on it as a naive and anxious young man. I boarded my Air France flight with a youthful imagination as to where my future would take me. Little did I know that much of it would come to fruition.

Chapter 12: City of Stars: July 1, 2022

As was agreed in my contract with Red Star, I had a new apartment in Saint-Denis to reside in while at the club. My grandfather tried his best to convince me to live with him, but I declined. He wasn't happy, but the truth was that I would be unable to live with my grandfather. I love him to death, and I plan on visiting him at every opportunity, but I need my space. He was worried about me losing myself in my fame, and he believed that living alone as a young man with a glamorized social status would predispose me to difficult and hedonistic situations. He was absolutely right, but my grandfather and I are from different worlds. We cannot understand each other's upbringings, paradigms or desires. Reality and time are daunting, and my perception of reality is extremely biased, nostalgic, flawed and inconsistent. I assured him that I would be okay, and he reluctantly conceded.

I was given a lot of affection upon my arrival back home. It quite literally felt like a dream. I don't mean that in the sense of the accomplishment of a long term goal, I mean it in the sense of an actual state of mind. I felt as if I was about to wake up at any moment. I had internalized a gloomy future and existence for so long that the manifestation of time being so different from what I expected has made some primal part of me feel offbeat, depersonalized and delusional.

My new teammates were very welcoming. Some of them mentioned some goals I had scored in America or my left foot. No one dared mention what I knew was certainly on their minds, my parents. They knew to leave that at the door. Truthfully, I would not be offended at anyone asking me about them. They are not me and I am not them. My understanding of the world I live in will always have sinister undertones but will never in and of itself be nefarious. Speaking from both a sense of nature and nurture, I am predisposed to a lot. I'm predisposed to intelligence, anger and quite fittingly, narcissism. I relish the idea that this was my fate. I relish the idea that I was meant to spill my soul into my journal, reflect about trauma that might only exist in my mind, close the notebook, and go on living a glamorous lifestyle. I relish the idea that I am crazy because in doing so, I romanticize my own insanity.

I spiral though. I lose myself inside my own head. I realize just how complex of a situation I am in and I realize my helplessness at learning more. I realize that learning more about reality would not make me happy, but I also realize that learning more about reality would likely render my happiness and my pursuit of it a fallacy to my predispositions. I realize that I will never figure that out, no matter what I do, because it is simply beyond what I can imagine.

This season was the first time that Red Star would be in the top flight of French football for a very long time. Our goal was clear: avoid relegation back to Ligue 2. Despite our common goal, the whole squad was a mix. Some of us were young players looking to prove themselves at the highest level, such as myself. Others were more established players to the French game, doing their best to keep their CV clean from a relegation; or for some, another relegation.

After getting a few jitters out in friendly appearances, I made my competitive debut for Red Star in the first match of the 2021-22 Ligue 1 season at home against Nantes. Nantes are a fairly reputable French club and were expected to finish mid-table. I was asked in the pre-match interview what impact I hoped to have on a Red Star team that would struggle to keep their head above water. Without hesitation I told the journalist that the ferocious passion I bring playing at home in front of my family and friends would scare any opposition. We both let out laughs, his definitely much more nervous than mine. My answer didn't have anything to do with my ability, what I was purchased for, or what he was expecting to hear. However, it was how I felt.

Coming out of the tunnel in that first match, I felt a spectacular rush. My family and friends no longer had to stay up at night tuning into sketchy Major League Soccer streams to watch me play. They were here. In the flesh. Sofiane, Ibrahim, Wissam, Mamadou, and of course, my grandfather. I couldn't wait to get out there and feel the floodlights fly into my eyes. I couldn't wait to keep writing that destined, miraculous, farfetched, masterpiece.

In regard to what I said in the interview, I held true to my word on my debut against Nantes. My teammates and I were able to be leading 2-0 going into the final minutes of the match thanks to a double from the club's star striker. With one of the last few kicks of the game, he cannoned another effort off the woodwork. It fell right in my stride on the edge of the box. I didn't even think to take a touch before redirecting the ball into the top left corner. The stadium roared as I wheeled away in celebration. I sprinted to my family and friends and in the front row and gave them a sweaty embrace. I walked back onto the pitch and relished the pure elation. 3-0. Game over. We were very proud of our dominant display, and I was very happy to score on my debut. As the full time whistle blew, I looked to the sky and wondered if they could see me. I shouldn't care. I don't want to care. But I always will.

Our dream start was quickly humbled. The following week, we were absolutely battered by Paris-Saint Germain, the reigning champions who were looking to claim their 5th successive title, and eighth in nine years. Despite the poor result, it was the first time I had been able to play against world class players. There were players on that PSG team that I had idolized as a kid and coming head to head against them was surreal.

A fairly stable run of form followed us into the autumn and winter months. By the end of November, we had played 14 matches out of the 38 total games in the season, and we occupied 18th place. In Ligue 1, the bottom two sides (20th and 19th) are automatically relegated, while the 18th place team plays a playoff match against the 3rd place team from the second division.

Our first match of December was away to iconic French club Olympique de Marseille. We took the train from Paris to Marseille in the south of France the day before the match. I was excited to visit Marseille. I had never been to the city, which is the second biggest in France. The Stade Velodrome was an incredible stadium, and I couldn't wait to display my magic on the perfectly cut grass.

I took in the atmosphere around the ground as I warmed up with my teammates. I had gotten to know them very well in the last few months. Many of the players on Red Star were of Maghrebi origin. I loved the guys I had played with in Seattle, but there was a strong cultural disconnect between a lot of us. It wasn't anyone's fault, but it made it difficult to properly assimilate into the squad. Here, I spoke the language, knew the city and understood the culture.

I usually warmed up with the left winger, a 23-year-old Parisian born, half Moroccan, half Turkish player named Ali. We had become close friends in my time here at Red Star. He had been in the Red Star academy since age 11 and broke into the first team a couple of years ago. On our days off, we often hang out at Sofiane's with the crew. He's a very generous man, but he's extremely bitter.

Ali is the youngest of four brothers, two of whom work at Red Star and one of whom is in jail on psychedelic drug charges. He negotiated jobs for his brothers into his first contract with the club. He tells me that they are extremely smart, and shouldn't be working as kit men and stewards, but they never had faith shown in them by their parents or the French system. I've met all three of his brothers. They are quite clearly conflicted, regretful and damaged from their poverty stricken and emotionally taxing past. They lost themselves inside their own minds, and their stories are all too similar to so many others from the banlieues of Paris. Ali maintains that he would be even more corrupted if it wasn't for his footballing ability and the faith Red Star had shown in him since he was a boy. He plays his heart out every match, and this has made him a fan favorite. He deserves all the praise he gets.

The match kicked off under the dusk sky at the Velodrome. It only took 14 minutes for the Marseille forward to latch onto the end of a cross and poke the ball past our keeper. It was 1-0 going into the break.

Early in the second half, Ali took on his man inside the box and was tripped up. It was a penalty kick. He stepped up and coolly placed it in the bottom right corner. Game on.

Marseille continued to dominate the match, as was expected. They were, however, struggling to break through. They struck the post twice in the 30 minutes following Ali's goal. The fans and players were clearly growing frustrated.

With 9 minutes remaining in the match, I received the ball just inside the Marseille half. I pinged a long ball with my left foot over to Ali on the other flank and began sprinting forward towards the back post. Ali whipped in a cross to our striker, but it flew over him and deflected off the defender right to me outside the 6 yard box. I prodded it home and yelled in ecstasy. The announcer at the stadium called out my name and number in a somber tone as Marseille rushed the ball back to the kickoff. Despite another few onslaughts of pressure towards our goal, we managed to scrape a huge win against one of the best sides in the league.

After our team dinner, I headed back to the hotel room. As soon as I entered the room, I heard my phone ring in my pocket. It was Mrs. Wilson. I answered right away.

"Zizou, what a goal! Lauren, my husband and I were watching the match on TV. We're very proud of you."

It truly did put a smile on my face to have the support of the Wilson's. I am so lucky to have met them. My dinner at their house will always be a pivotal moment in my life. I won't ever forget it. It helped shape me into who I was meant to be.

"Thank you, Mrs. Wilson, that means so much! I hope you're doing well. I miss you guys," I calmly replied.

"We're doing great! Listen, Zizou. Our granddaughter lives in Marseille. If you want to stop by and introduce yourself while you are in town, I think it would be really good for you and her. I can send you her address if you want?"

I did have an extra day off in Marseille and was curious at what their granddaughter was like. She was my age, and I had heard a lot about her.

"Absolutely, I would love to," I replied.

"Awesome, feel free to head over there in the afternoon tomorrow. Have a good evening Zinedine!" She said over the noisy, international connection.

"Same to you Mrs. Wilson."

I laid in my hotel bed with my headphones in and took it all in. I felt such extreme, inconsistent emotions. I pondered fate. I pondered the course of time and what it all meant to me. I pondered who I was and what mattered to me. No matter how successful I was, I couldn't let go of an extreme weight on my shoulders. I felt like I could hear the desperate screams of the victims of my parents every time the world went silent. I felt as if I could see their graves every time I closed my eyes. I felt ungrateful every time I felt anything other than bliss, which fuels a vicious cycle of frustration. I was living the dream, but when I was left alone with my thoughts and nothing to distract me from my dissociative and nihilistic tendencies, I still felt as if I was in a nightmare. I felt like a slave to my perspective, my past, and the poignant possibilities that were continuously being processed by my prefrontal cortex.

The next afternoon, I located the address that Mrs. Wilson had sent me. As I entered the apartment complex, I felt an overlying sense of significance associated with my actions. It wasn't pressure, it wasn't nerves, it wasn't even fear. It was as if destiny was trying to communicate with me, and it was only finding partial success. Very little of my future was outlined clearly, but I tried to trust my intuition. Such intuition seemed to place a profound importance on the decisions I was about to make.

I found unit #729 and knocked on the freshly painted door. After a few seconds, a short woman about my age opened the door. She had freckles and an AirPod protruding out of one of her noticeably small ears. Once her light brown eyes had scanned my face, she slammed the door in my face and locked it with the chain. So much for trusting my intuition.

I stood there for about a minute or so unsure of whether I should knock again or walk away. Such indecision struck me as an extremely prevalent metaphor for a lot of dilemmas that plague us in this life. I knew that the woman was Mrs. Wilson's granddaughter based on her features. She looked a lot like her grandma. Just as I was about to knock again, she unlocked the door and opened it. She signaled with her arm for me to come in. I took off my shoes and took a seat at the kitchen table.

"I'm sorry that I locked you out. Just seeing your face, and the fact that you look so much like him was a lot for me to handle. I'm sorry," she said in a high pitched, scratchy voice.

I didn't reply with words. I immediately got on my feet and gave her a huge hug. She held on tight and sunk her head into my shoulder. It was impulsive. It always hurts to internalize our similarities, but it hurts much more to know that they are still hurting her. I wanted to tear away my similarity to him with kindness.

"My name is Scarlett, but you know that already."

She laughed and took a seat in the chair next to me. I let out a chuckle and introduced myself.

"You lost me some money yesterday man. I bet on Marseille to win the game," she punched my arm jokingly, attempting to lighten the mood.

"What can I say?"

I shrugged and replied with a smile. I liked her energy. She had not stopped smiling since she introduced herself. Scarlett and I talked about everything. We started off talking about my career, and eventually shifted towards hers. She was doing online courses from the University of Washington, where Lauren had gone to college. By 2023, she hoped to have her B.A. in finance. In the meantime, she taught a girls' dance class in the city.

"You better do my taxes!" I sarcastically blurted out.

She nudged my shoulder and gave me a smile. Her smile was as sweet as honey. It was the most precious thing I had ever seen. I had just met her, but I never wanted to see that smile fade away. I never wanted to see tears in her eyes. I was never going to let anything happen to her.

Our conversation wandered around different aspects of our lives, stopping at every peaceful street and dangerous alleyway of our similar minds. We shared allegories of our childhood, shaping moments from our adolescence, our hopes and dreams, and our perspective. Eventually, our minds headed exactly where they were always destined to head.

"Zinedine, can I tell you a story?" She struggled to make eye contact with me as she said it.

"Of course," I gently replied.

"One time in middle school, this boy completely broke my heart. I mean, it was middle school, but still. I liked him so much, he was the most popular guy at our school and my hormonal brain told me that I really wanted to be with him. He led me on, feigning emotion, and eventually cut me off pretty abruptly. I really cared about him. I tend to really care about people even when they don't care about me."

"I'm sorry Scarlett, that really sucks," I replied.

"When I went home that day, my mom noticed I was down in the dumps. She asked me what was wrong, and I told her I was tired. She snarled back, telling me that life is tiring, that I didn't even know the half of it and that I better get used to it. That was the first time in my life I felt alone. I didn't feel like anyone could relate to me. I was left to my own devices. I had nowhere to turn."

I felt awful for her. I grabbed her hand. She continued.

"I've never been very close with my mom. You'd think we would have been inseparable, not having my father and all. Just the two of us. But she always acted like raising us was a chore. She acted like I was lucky she didn't die in the attacks, and that I should be showing her sympathy for the death of my father, despite the fact that I was a child. A child who had more trauma than most people go through in their lifetime."

I didn't know exactly where she was going with this tangent, but I was listening and would do anything to make sure she felt heard.

"I saw her get in abusive relationship after abusive relationship, I felt ashamed for being a burden on her. When I talk to other people, I always feel like I'm overcompensating, giving all of the love I have to give. I never understood why. When I dated boys, when I made friends, when I socialized, I always felt myself giving my all and never receiving the same energy. I had never experienced the unconditional love that I so often felt. I asked myself; do I care for people because I want to be cared for? If I had been cared for, would I be as good of a person? How can I even judge someone's morality looking at the world through those lenses?"

I nodded my head and let her continue. I really wanted to hear what she had to say. My eyes were locked with hers, my heart was beating with hers, and our minds were operating on the same wavelength.

"There are only two times I have experienced true, unconditional love. The first time was when I went to dinner at my grandparent's house in Seattle with Lauren. I had never met them before. My Mom didn't let me see them. By the time I turned 16 and my mom and I had already drifted apart. They flew me to Seattle and I got to meet them. They're my favorite people in the world. I love them with all my heart. I truly do."

"They're the best," I quickly said.

We gave each other a look full of emotion. It felt so special.

"The second time? Right now. I feel like you love me unconditionally. I know I just met you, but I can feel it. I know you wouldn't let me down. I feel understood. I feel trusted. I feel loved," she said wholeheartedly.

I had never felt the way that those words made me feel. It was an entirely new sensation. I had always been the enemy. I expected to be the enemy. This was one of the first times in my life that I was to be truly trusted by someone who was so recently a stranger. Although I knew she was right in doing so, the demons inside my head still told me that I would mess things up. I knew that I wouldn't be able to speak without my eyes watering up, and I desperately did not want to cry. I spread my arms out.

"Hug?" I said with a slight chuckle.

She laughed and gave me the biggest hug she could, which was still small because she was barely five feet tall.

Eventually, I had to catch the train back to Paris. I told her that she was welcome to come visit me in Paris whenever she wanted. She promised me we would keep in touch. I missed the lavender smell of her apartment and the innocent, yet damaged look in her beautiful brown eyes as I made my way to the train station. On the train, I felt myself forgetting my tragic condition. I felt myself forgetting the pain, I felt myself forgetting the sorrow of tomorrow, I felt myself forgetting the inconsistencies of this reality and losing myself in one specific consistency that exists within such reality. She was all I could think about. As I daydreamed, a track by Lupe Fiasco titled "Paris, Tokyo" spiraled through my headphones.

Mfu't hp up tmffq jo Qbsjt
Xblf vq jo Uplzp
Ibwf b esfbn jo Ofx Psmfbot
Gbmm jo mpwf jo Dijdbhp, nbo
Uifo xf dbo mboe jo uif npuifsmboe
Dbnfm-cbdl bdsptt uif eftfsu tboe
Boe ublf b usbjo, up Spnf, ps ipnf

Csbajm, gps sfbm

The track was a manifestation of my youthful exuberance. I wanted to travel the world, and in that moment on the rickety old train, I realized that I wanted that high pitched laugh next to me on every flight.

Upon my return to Paris, I called Lauren and told her that her niece was the most spectacular girl I had ever met. I couldn't help but smile while I said it. She laughed and told me she was really glad that we got along. I hung up the phone and fell right asleep.

The rest of the season was stressful. We all knew that our status as a Ligue 1 club would likely be decided on the final day of the season, and we all knew that one mistake could send us down. Going into the final matchday, we sat in 18th place, which would require us to play an extra playoff match for our survival. However, a home win against 16th place EA Guingamp would allow us to leapfrog them.

Ali scored the lone goal of the match in the 73rd minute. It was an extremely tight affair, and it could have gone either way. When the goal finally went in, the stadium nervously celebrated, knowing that his deflected shot might have provided salvation. I sprinted over to my friend and gave him a huge hug.

For the final minutes of the match, we defended with our lives. I had never been so motivated to track back, but this group of players and these fans deserved players who were willing to die for the badge. I knew I wasn't the only one who felt that way, and that collective courage was enough to see us over the line.

My stats for the season were fairly impressive. Eight goals and five assists for a young player in the French league was a quality return, and the club was very pleased with my contribution. We were all excited to reassemble the squad after our summer holiday and attempt to finish even higher up the table.

During my summer holiday, I spent just over half of my time at home in Paris. I played street soccer with my friends, I watched TV with my grandfather, I listened to Sofiane's stories. Despite the fact that everything had changed, nothing had truly changed at all. From a certain perspective, I feel as if that sentiment holds true for nearly every shift in our world, lives, and universe.

The remainder of my time was spent on a road trip with Wissam. We drove all the way through France and spent a week in Marseille, and another week in a nearby beach town called Palavas-les-Flots. I introduced him to Scarlett, and they immediately got along. The three of us spent our week in Marseille spending way too much money on clothes, enjoying dinners out at Scarlett's restaurants of choice in the city, and watching the whole series of *Avatar: The Last Airbender* at Scarlett's apartment. In Palavas, we rented a place from one of Wissam's family friends. Although slightly unprepared, it was cozy. We enjoyed the boardwalk, extravagant boat parties, watching the sunlight dwindle from the beaches of the Mediterranean, and ultimately made memories that will last a lifetime. By the end, I was fully refreshed and ready to return to Red Star.

When we dropped Scarlett back off in Marseille, I could barely stand saying goodbye. As I got to know her more, I began to get more and more attached. Everything she did made my heart skip a beat. She was everything I wanted. I gave her a kiss at her apartment and told her I'd be back. She laughed and told me she knew I would be.

Chapter 13: Lights Please: July 1, 2023

My start to the 2022-23 season was disastrous to say the least. We lost our opening four matches of the league, with one of those being a 1-0 loss due to an own goal I put into the net while defending a corner. By the fifth match, I was dropped to the bench. I was very disappointed in myself and had come down from the high of last season and my summer vacation. I was thrown back into the motions of real life. My friends tried to convince me that I was still making more money than all of them combined for kicking a leather ball around, but it only made me feel worse. I felt terrible for not performing. I knew that I had to kick on.

I watched our team suffer another loss in the fifth match of the season. Our sixth would be a date with PSG at the Parc de Princes. PSG had not been beaten in the league at their home stadium in over two years, and the bookies didn't reckon that a side with zero points would be the ones to do it.

As with every match I played in Paris, my crew and grandfather showed up to the stadium. They tell me stories about their discussions when watching me play. They talk about the reaction of the Red Star fans when I get the ball. I often hear that I am an entertaining player to watch. I struggle with inconsistency, but the supporters still get up out of their seats and onto their feet if they see me take a touch onto my left foot in the opposition's half. The idea that I could excite citizens that I don't even know by simply doing what I love makes me feel a massive amount of warmth. The thought that I was helping others' create the same nostalgic memories that fuel me was an elating realization.

Despite wave after wave of attack from the PSG superstars, our defence held strong. Our goalkeeper, a fellow French-Algerian named Samir was having the match of his life. The 22-year-old shot stopper had been a youth player at PSG for ten years before being released at 18 years old. He was getting revenge on his formative club by putting in his best ever display in professional football at the ground of his former employers.

With around ten minutes remaining in the match, Samir hoofed the ball forward into the PSG attacking third. Their central defender headed it only as far as my left foot about 40 yards from goal. I delicately took the ball out of the air and took him on with a roulette, just as my namesake, the great Zinedine Zidane used to do. Once I skipped past him, I was in on goal. Nearly the entire PSG team was pushed high up the pitch pressing for the opening goal. I sprinted with the ball towards the PSG keeper and poked the ball past him. The PSG supporters fell silent, but the Red Star fans who had traveled across town to watch the game were screaming in jubilation.

We conceded a corner in the dying seconds of the game, and I was the only attacking player left on the field for my team as the coach switched to a very defensive formation. At this point, even the PSG goalkeeper was up for the corner attempting to get an equalizer. The corner was whipped in and easily grasped by Samir. He punted the ball forward to me, and I easily took it towards the empty net and poked it in. 2-0 at the Parc des Princes. 2-0 against a club who would barely let me attend as a fan, let alone play in their ground only a half a decade ago. 2-0 against the club that released Wissam, leaving him to find himself on the streets. 2-0 for the Red Star fans who would be speaking of this match for years to come. 2-0 for Raphael, an Olympique Marseille supporter who viciously hated PSG, and who was looking down on me from heaven with a napoleon, some tea, and a smile.

The match against PSG gave me momentum that I had never experienced before. I felt as if I could take on the world, I felt everything fall into place inside of me. I was tuned out of reality, but it didn't matter. My instinct, my yearning to rewrite history, and my extreme tendency to chase and hide from emotion, whether it be the avoidance of pain or the pursuit of pleasure, spurred me on. In the 13 matches following the PSG game, I scored an incredible 15 goals as we sat comfortably in mid-table. One of those 15 strikes was a dazzling solo run and rocket into the top left corner against OGC Nice, a goal described by the Red Star ultras on social media as the greatest they had ever witnessed in their hallowed jersey. As a young player having my breakthrough season, I was beginning to attract interest from Europe's elite clubs. Going into the winter break, I was the top goal scorer in Ligue 1 and I had never felt better.

Life passed me by ever so quickly when things were going well. It made me contemplate the very persistence and illusion of time. When I was in that grey prison cell, time crawled past me slower than a sloth. Every day felt like a week, every week felt like a year, and the entire year felt like a lifetime. As I prospered, I wondered who was out there experiencing the same sensations I was in that prison cell. I often considered going and visiting the jail, but I couldn't bring myself to. I sat in that room with no hope for the future, a hyperaware understanding of my place in the human condition, and the understanding that such human condition was subjective, easy to manipulate, and could never be fully understood by anyone immersed in it. I looked to my ceiling and wondered if there was something more beyond that roof. Beyond the stars. Beyond my vision. Beyond my grasp. I don't wonder that much anymore. I don't chase anything beyond my worldly dreams much anymore. I don't need to, I don't want to. I am properly distracted. The elation that runs through my veins when I score a goal distracts me. The feeling I get when I see Scarlett smile distracts me. The understanding that I am fulfilling my grandfather's wishes distracts me. My past, and my subsequent future distracts me from the nagging feeling that everything I pondered in that prison cell was true, and that there is nothing I can do to change it. Maybe what I consider "distraction" from the ominous and harrowing nature of reality, existence, and everything within comprehension is all that life is meant to be? Maybe that is what makes it all worth it? I tend to ask myself questions about morality and the paradoxical nature of reality and morality in our modern world. It all comes back to perspective. My perspective was tragic, and now it's euphoric. My perspective is tribal, human and quite frankly primitive. And so is yours.

I tore up the rest of the season. I scored 10 more goals in the remaining 18 matches of the season, including another cracking long range effort in the home fixture against PSG. It felt like there was magic in my boots. There was no defender in the world who scared me. My on pitch performances felt like a parallel manifestation of my mental health. When I was feeling optimistic,

I translated that onto the pitch. Ever since I have had Scarlett in my life, ever since I have been able to give money back to my community and grandfather, I have felt full of happiness. I played with a smile, and I loved what I was doing. When I was down, I played poorly. I let my headspace affect my game.

I felt at home in Paris, but I was beginning to become a superstar. Red Star knew they would struggle to keep hold of me in the summer transfer window, and they were okay with that. They told me that they would not reject an offer less than 40 million euros, and I understood why. The inflation of the transfer market caused players like me to be priced out of big money moves, but I was not going to let Red Star sell me cheaply. They deserved to be able to renovate their squad with the money they received from any potential transfer, and if no bids came in that matched their asking price, I was happy to stay until they did. I am an ambitious player, but my loyalty trumps my ambition.

I didn't know exactly where I wanted to play. My agent, Munir Doukha encouraged me to move to England, as extremely lucrative salaries were available in the Premier League. I was open to the idea, but I wanted to wait and see what offers I would have on the table.

At the start of May, Munir gave me a call. I expected it to be about a potential transfer, but it wasn't. He told me that the Algerian FA wanted to inquire about my interest in representing the Algerian National Team at the upcoming 2023 African Cup of Nations in a month. He also told me that this interest prompted the French FA to inquire about my interest in representing *Les Bleus* in upcoming Nations League matches in September. I was absolutely stunned. I didn't know what I wanted. I hadn't visited

Algeria since I was a child, but I still felt a connection to the country stronger than I had ever felt with France. However, playing for France would elevate my status as a footballer and be historic for my family and for France itself. Honestly, it only took me five minutes to make up my mind. I would never forget how I felt when watching Algeria lift the 2019 AFCON only 4 years previous from the Delson Apartments. In a decision that stunned the French press, I rejected a French call up in favor of an Algerian call up. I had to rewrite history and diminish the shame my parents brought to my homeland. I had to do it. Not for the French, but for the Algerians. The Algerians who had died protecting their freedoms, and the Algerians who had suffered persecution all over the world following my parents' actions. I had to do it for them.

My decision didn't come without a lot of heavy interview questions about my political views. The far right in not only France but many countries had used my choice as an example of the threat that immigration poses, and to only further regurgitate my parents' story and the fact that I had "betrayed France". I told the press that the French only started to pay attention when I performed in America, and that I owe them nothing. This fueled the fire, and as a result, I made a lot of enemies amongst conservative French politicians and voters.

Going into AFCON, my Algeria side had a lot of pressure to perform. They had disappointed in the 2022 World Cup in Qatar, and we were looking to redeem ourselves in this African Cup. The only player I knew was Samir, my goalkeeper for Red Star, who had declared for Algeria six months previously. The rest of the squad was mostly made up of players from the Paradou academy in Algiers, or French-born Algerian players who had declared for the nation of their parents, such as myself. One of those players was a 32-year-old Riyad Mahrez. I told him about the influence he had on me and how inspired I was by his story, even when I was in jail. He laughed and told me that it was one of the most amazing things he had been told throughout his entire career. This meant a lot coming from an idol of mine, and someone who was possibly the most universally loved person in Algeria over the last decade.

The tournament was held in the Ivory Coast, however we completed our training in Algeria prior to the tournament. Traveling to Algeria was a mystical and profound experience. I immediately noticed how much work had to be done in the country. I immediately noticed the instability and trauma that plagued so much of the population. These people, especially those alive prior to 1962, had been through everything, but were still able to greet everyone with a smile on their face. Their perspective was so unexplainably different from those living in Paris, or especially Seattle. It was almost as if they were from different worlds. As soon as I walked in downtown Algiers and felt the vibrant and exuberant emotion, whether it was positive, negative, or a mixture of both, flowing through the streets of the capital, I knew I made the right decision in representing the Desert Foxes.

Despite the smiles, it was evident that something was deeply wrong in North Africa. Political turmoil and uncertainty had gripped the Maghreb at almost all moments since they gained their independence, even more so since the suicide of fruit vendor Mohamed Bouazizi in Tunisia in 2011, which sparked revolutions all across the Arab world. It was as Maghrebi as you could get; if you don't give me fair opportunity, I will light myself on fire. My desire to be free of oppression is stronger than my desire to continue to live in inequality. That was the message that Bouazizi left his country and the world with when he lit himself on fire after being assaulted and criticized by the same government officials who kept him, and most other young men, unemployed.

Traveling to sub-Saharan Africa for the tournament was also a unique experience. The people in Algeria and Ivory Coast hated France and what France did to them, but if you offered them a one-way ticket to Paris, they would bite your hand off. It was clear to see the dysfunction and toxicity that the colonization of Africa had caused, even more than half a century later.

We performed very poorly in the tournament, failing to get out of the group stage. The vibe was entirely different than in Europe. I failed to get a goal or an assist as we lost to Nigeria and the DR Congo and drew against Guinea. Ivory Coast were the eventual champions in their homeland, and our squad was full of Algerian rage on our flight home. We had bonded as a team, but we were full of regret. For some of these players, they would never get to represent Algeria again. I hoped that wasn't the case for me, but it reminded me that happy endings are only for the lucky few and are all based on your paradigm. For some, even putting on that jersey would be a dream come true. For some, even playing football with a pumped ball would be a dream come true. For some, even the very distasteful airplane food we were fed on our way back would be a dream come true. It reminded me how ungrateful we are, and how accustomed we become to our surroundings.

Despite our poor results, it was still the greatest moment of my career thus far to represent Algeria. It was controversial to say the least, even being cited in a question about foreign policy with former French colonies and the French born children of North African immigrants in the French presidential debate. Nonetheless, pulling on the green and white Algeria jersey and representing my grandfather, my ancestors and the Algerian people was indescribable responsibility and honor.

After the tournament, I traveled to Germany, Spain and England to analyze potential destinations. I had offers from Crystal Palace, a midtable Premier League side in London, Atletico Madrid, a huge Spanish club, Borussia Dortmund, a German side that plays exciting, attacking football with quick, young players, and FC Barcelona, a side who were the best team in the world for most of my life. Ever since they lost Lionel Messi in 2022, a player who is often regarded as the best in history, they had fallen from their once great heights. Crystal Palace were offering the most money, and I desperately wanted to live in London, but the squad was not strong enough in comparison to the other clubs. Atletico Madrid had solidified themselves as one of the best teams in the world in the last decade, but many players with similar profiles to myself had failed at the club, and I didn't enjoy the vibe of Madrid or the defensive football they played. In my head, it was between Dortmund and Barcelona. My grandfather told me to go for Barcelona. He recalled the incredible Barcelona teams that he had seen throughout the 20th century and early 21st century and told me how amazing it would be to see me wearing that famous blaugrana kit. Sofiane and my friends told me to go for Dortmund, as they had a wonderful track record for developing players such as myself into global superstars. I was conflicted and felt a heavy weight on my shoulders.

I pulled out my phone and called Scarlett. I hadn't spoken to her at all about the transfer negotiations. All she knew was that I was likely to move clubs in the summer.

As soon as she picked up, I immediately dropped the question,
"Do you want to move to Dortmund or Barcelona?"

She let out an adorable laugh and stayed silent for a good 20 seconds before saying Barcelona.

Later that week, I was being unveiled at the legendary Camp Nou stadium in Barcelona as a 44 million euro transfer. Scarlett was in the front row and so was my grandfather. I hadn't introduced the two of them before this. My grandfather insisted that I either marry her or rent a separate apartment nearby for her until we got married. We were still young, and she was apprehensive at the thought of that commitment, so I rented her the next door apartment to please my grandfather and his Islamic requirements. I was still Muslim and attended *Jumuah* prayer every week. Scarlett wasn't an atheist but was not religious. As far as my grandfather was concerned, she was a very smart girl who had great manners, and who knew how to cook Maghrebi food. She treated him with a lot of respect, and Scarlett told me after the unveiling that they went shopping in downtown Barcelona and spoke about embarrassing things I did as a kid while I was sorting out my paperwork at the club. I was happy that she was becoming part of the family. She meant everything to me. More than this multi-million dollar contract, more than this lavish apartment, more than my heartbreaking past. From my perspective, everything was dwarfed by her smile.

Chapter 14: Stronger: July 1, 2024

Life in Barcelona was immeasurably different than anything I had ever experienced before. I had become a celebrity and couldn't avoid the limelight. Every time I showed myself in public, I was signing shirts and snapping selfies. Scarlett and I loved the city. We spent our free evenings wandering downtown and eating the lamb chops at *Restaurant A La Turka*. We loved to go on spontaneous excursions, hopping in the car after dinner and driving towards the sunset with no designated destination. We loved to turn the radio up and listen to "Blinding Lights" by The Weeknd, a euphoric track that she could not get enough of.

> J tbje, ppi, J'n cmjoefe cz uif mjhiut
> Op, J dbo'u tmffq voujm J gffm zpvs upvdi
> J tbje, ppi, J'n espxojoh jo uif ojhiu
> Pi, xifo J'n mjlf uijt, zpv'sf uif pof J usvtu
> Ifz, ifz, ifz

However, even in my most relaxed moments, I felt disillusioned in relation to my expectations. My heavy price tag was weighing on my shoulders. 44 million euros. That was outrageous money. I knew that I was worth it, but a troubling voice inside my head liked to ask me; what if you let everyone down? What if you flop? At first, I did everything off the pitch to remedy the voice. I put on headphones, I watched Netflix with Scarlett. After that didn't work and I started to perform well in our first training sessions, I realized that the only thing that would shut it up was by proving it wrong.

Wandering around Camp Nou and the Joan Gamper Training Center was otherworldly. This was where some of the best of all time had given football fans iconic memories. Maradona, Ronaldinho, Messi, Xavi, Iniesta, Cruyff, and so many more. I couldn't wait to hear the fans sing the club anthem as I took to the field.

The truth was that FC Barcelona was not the same as it had been when I was growing up. At the peak of their powers between 2008 and 2015, FC Barcelona had been famed for having the best youth academy in the world. They dismantled world football with players that they had nurtured since they were children. However, ever since their 2015 UEFA Champions League win, they had been spending big money on players such as myself and neglecting the players in their own academy. Many of those players had gone on to have stunning careers elsewhere, leaving Barcelona fans frustrated with the board. This frustration continues to exist and means that many supporters were not as intrigued with my transfer as they likely could have been.

Either way, I had given possibly the biggest shoes in football history and had been told to fill them. Rosario born forward Lionel Messi had played on the right wing for Barcelona from 2006 until 2022. He had been the best player in the world for most of the last two decades and was arguably the greatest player of all time. No matter how well I did at the club, I would never be able to live up to him and I knew that when I accepted the contract.

Unfortunately, in my first few matches, you wouldn't have even known I was playing the same sport as the great Argentine. I felt extremely off the pace. I was the only new acquisition the Barcelona first team had made this summer, and it was clear that I was the odd one out. I struggled to adapt to their possession based philosophy, and the fans were jumping on the hate bandwagon after only four matches. Scarlett told me that she knew I would prove them wrong, but inside my brain, her support only got quieter as the voice got louder.

My first goal finally came at the Camp Nou in October against relegation-threatened CD Leganes, but the fans barely even cheered my trademark, curling left-footed strike. I had always felt disconnected from my timeline, from my reality, from my very existence. However, football had been the lifeline that reality had thrown at me. It felt like I had pulled too hard and the line had snapped, leaving me in a completely different world. The fans and my teammates were on a different wavelength from me.

I still had the support of the Algerian fans until I failed to perform against Tanzania and Gabon in World Cup Qualifiers in November, matches we lost and drew respectively. These upsets meant that we would not be eligible to play in the 2026 World Cup, a tournament we were expected to compete in. Football fans had excruciatingly short memories, and just as my lack of youth football and consistency had been erased from the minds of the Sounders and Red Star fans, my performances in Seattle and in Paris had been erased from minds of the Barcelona and Algeria fans. By February 2025, I was dropped from the Barcelona starting lineup and was only making cameo appearances from the bench. My grandfather blamed the club's hierarchy for how they managed me, but I knew this one was on me. I just could not live up to the expectation. The pressure broke me down, and I wasn't relaxed enough to perform. It was disheartening, and I tried not to think about it, because when I did, I fell apart.

By March, Scarlett had been traveling back and forth to Marseille to visit her Mom, who had terminal cancer. I tried to go with her over the winter break, but her mother did not want to meet me. Just from the way Scarlett talked about her visits, and her tone of voice on the phone when with her mother, I could sense the dysfunction of their relationship and how much it subconsciously shaped Scarlett, and that hurt me deeply. I wished her mother the best not only because she had been through a lot in her life and of course because she was Scarlett's mom, but also because she reminded me of my parents and what they did. Maybe it was selfish for me to want to distance myself from that and no longer face those demons, but thinking about all of that and what it did to so many like Scarlett's mom is too heartbreaking for me to contemplate for more than a few minutes. My humanity will not allow it.

In early April, she decided to go back to Marseille for good. Her mother probably wouldn't make it to the end of the month. Once she passed away, she told me that she needed some time to figure things out. It wasn't a breakup in the traditional sense, because we still talked every day. However, as the weeks passed us by, we spoke less and less. I gave more in an effort to keep her, but by the start of June, she cut me off. I was left all alone.

I opened the door to my Barcelona apartment and the hardwood floor felt as cold as my heart. Nothing mattered anymore. I was full of frustration. My vision was blurrier than my past and my soul was left clawing at thin air. My happy ending had come to a halt.

Perspective fuels absolutely everything. It wasn't a matter of being grateful, it was a matter of psychology. I had millions of dollars and millions of fans, but my heart was more empty than it had ever been. I couldn't focus on football. I couldn't focus on anything. I missed her more than I could even articulate. Salty tears streamed out of my eyes every night for most of the summer, and despite the fact that no one was around to see them, I still felt ashamed at the fact that I was unable to control my emotions.

I felt as if I was perpetually running in circles. I couldn't get her smile out of my head. Life became gloomy, lonesome and heartbreaking. Life became tragic, tiring and incomplete. Life became lifeless. "Los Ageless" by St. Vincent often soothed my shattering memories of her. The eerily familiar production seemed to tap into the same nostalgia she created, giving me at least a moment of relief and connection to better times.

Ipx dbo bozcpez ibwf zpv?
Ipx dbo bozcpez ibwf zpv boe mptf zpv?
Ipx dbo bozcpez ibwf zpv boe mptf zpv
Boe opu mptf uifjs njoet, upp?
Ipx dbo bozcpez ibwf zpv?

Ipx dbo bozcpez ibwf zpv boe mptf zpv?

Ipx dbo bozcpez ibwf zpv boe mptf zpv

Boe opu mptf uifjs njoet?

In late June, the Barcelona board told me I would be sold in the summer. My adventure in the capital of Catalonia did not last long. In hindsight, it felt more like a vacation gone wrong and less like a dream move for my career. I never even got to play in a match against our famous rivals, Real Madrid. My confidence was shattered, and my happiness was lost to time.

The Spanish and French press had published stories about a loan move back to Red Star, or a transfer to Olympique Marseille. I didn't want either of those things. I needed a fresh start, a fresh perspective, and a fresh mind. A few weeks after the transfer window opened, I had been notified of interest from Arsenal, a huge club in London that had been performing well below the expectations of the fans for many years. Their famous red badge, which was described by their representatives as scarlet, reminded me of her every time I looked at it. I flew to London to meet their newly appointed manager, who was none other than my namesake, Zinedine Zidane.

The classy man called me into his office. He was wearing a navy blue suit, and his presence felt absolutely unreal. Despite the fact that I had been accustomed to the superstardom that came with being a famous footballer, I still had a nostalgic and ethereal view of the great Zinedine Zidane. I nervously took a seat in front of him. In French, he started discussions.

"Zinedine, what do you want to do with the rest of your career?"

I thought about presenting the formulated response, telling him that I want to win trophies for Arsenal Football Club and give my all for the badge. The truth was, I just wanted to make my family proud and build myself a legacy. Hopefully in the process I could gain the support of the fans and help the club, but more than anything, I wanted to prove my doubters wrong. The French media used my poor form to attack me, and many in France called me a "one-season wonder". I wanted more than anything to make those comments look silly.

"I want to make my family and friends proud." I blurted out.

Zidane looked right into my eyes. He got out of his chair and stood up, towering over his desk. He asked me a question.

"Do you not feel you have already done that?"

I took a second to think about it. Everything I had been through. Every time I kept running on the pitch even when I thought I had absolutely nothing left to give. Every time I kept running through life even when I thought I had absolutely nothing left to give. Every time I doubted myself and was able to persevere. All of the obstacles that stood between an unpolished, villainous teenager from Barbés and Zinedine Zidane. He didn't let me reply.

"I promise you that you have made your family proud and will continue to make your family proud."

I wanted to reply that I had failed in Barcelona, but he provided his response to that before I could get a word in.

"Don't tell me you failed in Barcelona. You remember the World Cup final I won? Now remember the one I got sent off in and lost. You remember the Champions' League I won? Now remember the two I lost. You didn't fail in Barcelona. You learned in Barcelona. Here, you will apply what you learned, and we will win everything together."

There was absolutely no greater honor than hearing those words of encouragement come from the magician himself. I immediately stood up and shook his hand. He displayed his signature smile.

A few days later, I was signing for Arsenal in a 12 month loan deal from Barcelona. The Gunners had the obligation to make the loan deal permanent for 25 million pounds if I played more than 10 full matches for them.

I moved to London alone and rented a townhouse in the north of the city. The weather as well as the general "distant friendliness" of the citizens reminded me of my time in Seattle. It had a slightly science-fiction, dystopian feel to it. That's not to say London wasn't brilliant. I absolutely loved the diversity and overall charm to the environment. However, it felt different than any other major city I had visited. It was mysterious, ominous, and vibrant all at the same time. I was ready to take it by storm.

PUMA sent me a scarlet undershirt to wear under my Arsenal top. Every moment that I had to myself, I thought about her. I would give anything to have her in my arms. I knew she was thinking about me too, and I knew she was wondering what was going on in my head. I knew that I had to move on, and I knew that the best way to do that would be to absolutely tear up the best football league on the planet, the English Premier League.

On my first night in my new place, I laid in bed alone with my nightmare of Barcelona still close and Scarlet still far. "Stronger" by Kanye West played on the speakers in my place. Everything had fallen apart, but I was ready to put it back together.

> O‑opx ui‑uibu uibu epo'u ljmm nf
> Dbo pomz nblf nf tuspohfs
> J offe zpv up ivssz vq opx
> 'Dbvtf J dbo'u xbju nvdi mpohfs
> J lopx J hpu up cf sjhiu opx
> 'Dbvtf J dbo'u hfu nvdi xspohfs
> Nbo, J'wf cffo xbjujoh bmm ojhiu opx
> Uibu't ipx mpoh J cffo po zb
> (Xpsl ju ibsefs, nblf ju cfuufs
> Ep ju gbtufs, nblft vt tuspohfs)
> (J offe zpv sjhiu opx!)
> (J offe zpv sjhiu opx!)
>
> Zpv lopx ipx mpoh J'wf cffo po zb
> Tjodf Qsjodf xbt po Bqpmmpojb
> Tjodf P.K. ibe Jtpupofst

Epo'u bdu mjlf J ofwfs upme zb

Epo'u bdu mjlf J ofwfs upme zb

Epo'u bdu mjlf J ofwfs upme zb

Epo'u bdu mjlf J ofwfs upme zb

Epo'u bdu mjlf J ofwfs upme zb

Chapter 15: Going Through Changes: April 14th, 2025

Living alone was a freeing experience. My room was a mess, the dishes were piling up in the sink, and I was never home. I did what I had always done, wander the city and take everything in. I liked to meander through the picturesque London streets with "Lover is a Day" by CUCO playing in my headphones. The soft and playful production felt directly tied to an unspecific, seductive sentiment stuck inside my soul.

Ujnf dibohfe, xf'sf ejggfsfou

Cvu nz njoe tujmm tbzt sfevoebou uijoht, dbo J opu uijol?

Xjmm zpv mpwf uijt qbsu pg nf?

Nz mpwfs jt b ebz J dbo'u gpshfu

Gvsuifsjoh nz ejtubodf gspn zpv

Sfbmjtujdbmmz, J dbo'u mfbwf opx

Cvu J'n plbz bt mpoh bt zpv lffq nf gspn hpjoh dsbaz

Lffq nf gspn hpjoh dsbaz

...

J'mm ublf uif cvnqz spbe, ju'mm qspcbcmz csfbl nz mfht

Bt mpoh bt J epo'u tipx zpv xibu't svjojoh nz ifbe

Gvooz uijoh bcpvu zpv jt zpv sfbe nf qsfuuz xfmm

Cvu zpv ibwfo'u gpvoe nf zfu bu uif cpuupn pg uif xfmm

Boopzjoh zpv xjui tnplf tjhobmt, btljoh zpv gps ifmq

'Dbvtf zpvs jnnfejbuf qsftfodf mjgut nf tusbjhiu bxbz
gspn ifmm

Nf boe Ns. Ifbsu, xf tbz uif dvuftu uijoht bcpvu zpv
Ipx zpv tffn vosfbm boe xf'e qspcbcmz ejf tp rvjdl
xjuipvu zpv
Tvggpdbufe gspn uif sbejbufe bjs bspvoe vt
Gvmm pg ibqqjoftt xf epo'u ibwf, csjhiuoftt hpof
Tp ebsl xjuipvu zpv, hjsm

Little things reminded me of her, but I was slowly healing. What hurt me most was the fact that Scarlet told me when I met her that no one ever loves her as much as she loves them. Ironically, I love her more than she loves me, or at least more than she can express. It really killed my self-confidence, and I was desperately attempting to get it back before the season started.

Slowly but surely, my stress and sorrow turned into motivation and determination to come back stronger. No one remembers those who wilted under the pressures of life. No one remembers the man who let them tear him apart, whether that is in reference to Scarlett, time itself, or both.

In August, I made my debut at the famous Emirates Stadium in North London in a match against my former suitors, Crystal Palace. I came off the bench with the match square at 1-1 and 23 minutes left to play. I threw on my vivid violet PUMA cleats and ran onto the pitch.

This match was Arsenal's second of the season. The first match was a 3-2 away win against newly promoted Leeds United.

Arsenal had finished 9th in the previous year, which was horrendous for their naturally high standards. However, after spending a combined total of 200 million euros this summer, big things were expected of Zinedine Zidane and his squad.

I played very well in my first 10 minutes as an Arsenal player. I felt more confident than I ever had in a Barcelona jersey. I was skipping past defenders and slotting my teammates passes.

With 5 minutes remaining in the match, Portuguese winger Rui Faria whipped the ball into the danger zone. The Crystal Palace defender cleared it only as far as my outstretched foot at the edge of the box. I took a touch to control the ball, then another to meg the Crystal Palace player who cleared it. The fans screamed in awe. I calmly tucked the ball past the goalkeeper, giving my side the lead and scoring my first goal. The supporters were up on their feet, and I sprinted to the TV camera to celebrate. I knew she was watching. I pointed to the color on my sweaty jersey and gave a seductive, albeit desperate wink.

I was once again able to score in our next match, an away win against Everton. The final score was 2-0, and I was man of the match, with a left footed finish for the first goal as well as an assist from a cross. My foot was on the gas pedal, and I was not going to let anything stop me.

Our next match was a critical one, the North London Derby against Tottenham Hotspur. Tottenham and Arsenal are bitter rivals, and often play out fiery battles on the football pitch. The Emirates stadium was jam packed, and I was in the starting lineup. I couldn't wait to get out there. Zinedine Zidane did a very good job managing us as players. We all wanted to fight for him on the pitch, and we all understood our role in the system and were happy to give our all.

Tottenham were the favorites despite being the away side. Arsenal hadn't beat them in over a year, and we were all fired up and raring to go. Unfortunately, this enthusiasm led our central defender into a rash tackle in our own penalty box in the opening minutes of the game. The referee pointed to the penalty spot, and the Tottenham captain stepped up and converted. We had an uphill battle ahead of us.

We dominated possession for the remainder of the first half, but struggled to carve out any clear cut chances. After the break, we got back out onto the field and were determined to comeback. I felt connected to the energy of my teammates, something I hadn't truly felt in Barcelona. We were ready to give everything to achieve our goals, and even when that was not enough, we would dig deeper and find more.

In the 66th minute, I robbed a Tottenham defender of possession and found myself in on goal. I lashed a shot past the keeper, but it struck off the post. I was furious with how close I had come but knew that I would get another chance. Only two minutes later, I received a pass from our central midfielder in a similar position to where I had won the ball previously. I beat the defender in front of me with a few precise body feints, and delicately curled the ball past the keeper. The fans chanted my name as I wheeled away in celebration. There are only so many words you can use to describe that rush of adrenaline you feel when you put the ball in the back of the net. It is distinct, special and addictive.

In the 73rd minute, the ball fell to me on the right flank after a scrap in the midfield. I started dribbling towards the full back and cut inside with a chop. Without thinking, I mercilessly smashed the ball on frame. The shot caught the goalkeeper off guard and was too powerful for his reach. We took the lead, and when the full time whistle blew, I had written myself into Arsenal folklore.

After our match against Tottenham, we sat at the summit of the Premier League table. Arsenal hadn't won the Premier League in 20 years and were predicted to finish 6th. We were ready to prove the bookies wrong.

Following that goal, I began to have the season of my life. Everything in football is about momentum. Once you get going, whether that is in a training session, match, or season, no one can stop you. You can train your technique forever, you can do everything you can to prepare yourself, but sometimes it just comes down to the unconscious reward system of your brain to fuel your brilliance.

By Christmas, I had racked up 14 goals and 7 assists in 18 games, which were described by pundit Jermaine Jenas as "undoubtedly world class statistics". I had also scored my first goal for the Algeria national team in a November clash against Libya in Oran, the hometown of my grandfather. I couldn't help but look to the creamy, Maghrebi sky once I blasted the ball into the net. I dedicated that goal to my grandmother, who was buried not too far from the stadium. My grandfather told me that she would have been so proud of the young man I was becoming. I couldn't help but tear up when I heard those words.

We lingered in 2nd going into 2025, only 2 points off of the league leaders Chelsea. We managed to beat them 3-2 at Stamford Bridge on January 19th. I racked up two assists in the match and scored a winning volley in injury time. After going ballistic with the away supporters in the celebration, I made sure to mouth happy birthday to Scarlett on the television camera. Despite my success on the pitch, I still thought about her every night before I went to sleep. I still missed her smile, her laugh, her presence. I still listened to "Blinding Lights" on the speakers at my place, but the numb comfort I had previously felt had transformed into numb sorrow.

> J'wf cffo po nz pxo gps mpoh fopvhi
> Nbzcf zpv dbo tipx nf ipx up mpwf, nbzcf
> J'n hpjoh uispvhi xjuiesbxbmt
> ...
> Op pof't bspvoe up kvehf nf (Pi)
> J dbo'u tff dmfbsmz xifo zpv'sf hpof
> ...
> J tbje, ppi, J'n cmjoefe cz uif mjhiut
> Op, J dbo'u tmffq voujm J gffm zpvs upvdi
> J tbje, ppi, J'n espxojoh jo uif ojhiu
> Pi, xifo J'n mjlf uijt, zpv'sf uif pof J usvtu

At this point, I was cementing myself as not only one of the best players in England, but the world. I wasn't sure how it happened. I wasn't sure how long it would last, but I was doing everything I could to relish and prolong the pleasure.

I brought the crew to London all the time. Mamadou, Wissam, Ibrahim, Sofiane and my grandfather were here almost as much as they were in Barbés. We wasted my money on the clothes and meals we always said we would as teenagers. I loved those days more than anything else in my life, and those were the moments from my career and ultimately my entire life that would flash before my eyes as I passed on.

In April, we held the cards in the title race. Wins against Manchester City and Tottenham once again put us in pole position to claim the trophy. The night after our match against Tottenham at White Hart Lane, I returned home and crashed onto my bed. I was exhausted, but let adrenaline carry my sore limbs through each fixture.

Just as I was about to fall asleep, I heard a faint knock on my wooden door. I wondered who it could possibly be. I stayed in bed, deciding that it likely wasn't as important as my rest. I began to doze off once more, and just as I began to lose consciousness, the knock returned with more urgency to it. I slowly got out of bed and walked towards the door. As I got closer, I felt a flashback to the day in which the law enforcement knocked on my grandfather's door and told him I would go to prison. I shivered slightly as I put my hand on the doorknob recalling the trauma. I creaked open the door, and as I looked down, I saw those piercing brown eyes staring at me. Before I knew it, I was receiving the tightest hug I could imagine, and tears were streaming out of my distinguishable eyes. I was overcome with emotion.

"What are you doing here?" I said in a confused tone.

"Fixing a mistake I made," she said matter of factly before leaning in and giving me a kiss.

I was overwhelmed with confusion, elation and suspicion. Her arrival at my door was straight out of a romcom. I threw on some clothes and we went for a walk through the dark London streets.

"I should've never left you Z. I missed you so much. I'm so sorry." She looked at me with the same googly eyes as the iPhone emoji. I grabbed her small hand and interlocked it with mine. Logically, I should have been more weary than I was, but I knew Scarlett. I knew her as well as I knew myself. I knew how hard it was for her to come here, and I knew that I needed to trust her. She could barely get a sentence out without her pupils watering up.

We strolled through the city, speaking as if nothing had ever happened at all. She told me her mother had told her to break up with me. She told me that she didn't think she deserved the unconditional love I gave her. She told me that it is and was her biggest fear that she would mess that up.

Everyone in my life would tell me I was better off leaving her in my past; but I couldn't help letting her go. Some things feel meant to be. Some things are worth the pain. Some things are worth being vulnerable for.

Life felt perfect as we walked down the deteriorating sidewalk. I was never going to let her go.

Chapter 16: Mama Africa: July 12, 2025

By early May, Chelsea had fallen off in the title hunt and we sat a comfortable 7 points ahead of them. Only a handful of games remained, and we had the opportunity to win the elusive Premier League title on my 24th birthday.

May 9th, 2025 set the date for our home match against 10th place Everton Football Club. A win would mean that the Premier League title would finally come back to North London.

In the 31st minute, Kosovan international defender Ardian Sadriu put us in the lead after latching onto a corner kick. It was his first goal of the season, and it was an incredible time to get it. The Arsenal supporters began to lose themselves in the moment.

With only 5 minutes remaining, Everton were throwing everyone forward in the hopes of netting an equalizer, but it wasn't coming. Sadriu dished me a through ball into space, and I rounded the Everton keeper and passed it into the empty net for my 26th goal of the Premier League season. As soon as the full time whistle rang in our ears, the stadium erupted in celebration unlike anything I have ever seen in my career. I looked to Scarlett in the front row and gave her the same wink I did through the TV cameras months earlier. She kicked her legs in excitement and blew me a kiss. Life could not get any better.

That summer, I would get the opportunity to compete in the African Cup once again. This time, the tournament was to be played in Guinea, and I was ready to win more silverware.

Coming off of the back of the season I had just had, in which I won the Premier League Player of the Year amongst multiple other personal accolades, all eyes were on me as the teams prepared to compete for the iconic trophy.

I took Scarlett with me to Guinea, and I flew my grandfather, Sofiane and the crew from Paris as well. I had a special feeling about the tournament, and I wanted them to be there. My grandfather had some complications with his diabetes earlier that year but was still in incredible health *alhamdulillah*. He was to celebrate his 77th birthday a day before the final.

I scored 4 goals in the 3 group stage matches as we swept our bracket and qualified for the Round of 16. We comfortably disposed of hosts Guinea in the last 16 and faced Senegal in the quarter finals. I scored the lone goal of the match, a long distance strike in the 111th minute of extra time to send the Algeria fans into absolute raptures. As always when playing with my national team, I looked to the sky and wondered if they could see me. Ironically, I was spreading a more positive image of Islam to the world than my parents did, and they sold their souls for it.

A comfortable 3-1 win against fellow Maghrebi side Tunisia in the semi-finals spurred us onto a date with our bitter rivals Egypt in the final.

The rivalry between Algeria and Egypt is one of the most heated in the entire world. So much so that extra military reinforcement in each of the nations had been prepared in order to maintain order ahead of the historic match. Both nations had extremely passionate fans, and millions of viewers across the globe were excited to see such a spirited affair.

The atmosphere ahead of the game was cinematic. As I walked out of the tunnel onto the pitch, I knew the historical implications. If we won, Algerians would tell their children and grandchildren about the great team of 2025, spearheaded by the son of the enemy. It was tremendous pressure, and I had folded under less pressure before in Barcelona, but I threw my experience in Spain out of my head and knew I was destined to make history. I thought of all the young boys and girls in the banlieues of Paris watching the game, forgetting about their poverty stricken condition to tune in and watch their heroes take to the field. I had to do it for them.

The match was scrappy for the first 75 minutes of the 90. A red card had been shown to each side, and the referee had to break up multiple altercations. Every tackle was studs up, and my leg was full of scrapes and bruises. Each of the teams were defending with extreme passion and organization.

In the 77th minute, American-born Egyptian winger Kareem Helal whipped in a corner kicked which veteran Mohamed Salah latched onto the end to put his side into the lead, breaking Algerian hearts, including mine. I dropped my head, but as soon as I looked out at my grandfather in the stands with his head in wrinkly hands, I screamed at my defenders to get the ball. I would not accept defeat.

After 5 minutes of Algerian onslaught, Marseille born Salim Aroul danced past his man in the middle of the park and took his space. I screamed for the ball on the right flank. He played it to me, and I skipped past my defender and found myself on the edge of the box. I faked another shot and zigzagged my way past another defender about a foot taller than myself. Without hesitation, I hammered the ball past the Egyptian goalkeeper. 1-1. Game on. In my head, I could hear those kids back home erupt in celebration. It was a unique and sweeping experience.

As regulation time concluded, we prepared for extra time. If we could not be separated in extra time, the match would have to go to a dreaded penalty shootout. Luckily for me, it wouldn't. In the 104th minute, full back Youcef Atal rushed down the wing. There were two Egyptian defenders chasing him, but Atal's blistering pace allowed him to carry the ball to the byline and square a ball to me at the edge of the box. The whole world slowed down as that ball came to me. This would be a moment that could go down in the history of my nation. A million things swirled around my psyche as the ball fell to me, but none of it mattered. I whacked the ball with my outstretched right foot off the post and into the back of the net. I sprinted to my grandfather and gave him a wink. My teammates piled on top of me and we sang in celebration.

At the final whistle, I fell to the floor in exhaustion and triumph. I lifted the cup towards the African stars on that magical night, with millions of Algerians screaming in unison with me. Tears streamed down my battered and bruised face. We had conquered our rivals. We had conquered our past. We had conquered Africa.

Chapter 17: Guerilla: July 13, 2030

It has been five years since our triumph in Guinea. Following the tournament, I went on to win 2 more Premier Leagues, an FA Cup, a UEFA Champions League Final against FC Barcelona, and a Ballon D'or, the award for the best footballer in the world in any given calendar year. I went down as an Arsenal legend and won everything there was to win in club football. I was injured for the entirety of the 2028-29 season, which is when I married Scarlett. We had our ups and downs, but she was the only person I had ever met who always knew how to make me smile. From a reductionist viewpoint, Scarlett and football were the two loves of my life. They saved me. With just one of them, I wouldn't be fulfilled. With both? I lose myself in this absurd and irrational human condition and everything feels okay.

We invited everyone to our wedding in Marseille. I hunted everyone who had ever impacted me down and paid for their travel and hotel. It truly was a sight to see all of them in the same place. Former teammates from all of my clubs, the now retired Coach Stuart Hill. Anthony, the man who had sat next to me on my first flight to the United States. Even Houari, my prison roommate, who was rehabilitated following his release and now worked as a mechanic. Scarlett invited just as many as I did, and it was the best day of our lives. We rented out an entire resort for the wedding. It was lavish, gorgeous, and ultimately perfect. The July sky was beautiful, and the view of the Mediterranean with everyone I loved around me would never be recreated or forgotten. I wished you could show a video of that wedding to me while I was in my prison cell. I would probably ask you where you got all the money for such incredible video editing software.

In the 2027 African Cup, we fell to a Nigeria side in the semi-finals that inevitably lost to the Egyptians in the final. The 2029 African Cup of Nations was hosted in Algeria, and we went on to reclaim our title on home soil, beating our neighbors Morocco 2-0 in the final. One of those strikes was a left footed free kick I hammered into the roof of the net.

I played the 2029-30 season on loan at Red Star. Despite the fact that I was a critical player for Arsenal and in the prime of my career, my grandfather's health was starting to deteriorate. I didn't need more trophies. I knew I had to move home and spend as much time with him as possible while I still could. I accepted a pay cut to return to Red Star, even rejecting a mouthwatering contract from PSG to remain loyal to the club who gave me my big break in European football.

My season was numerically impressive. I scored 19 goals in 18 games in the French league, alongside winning the French Cup. This title was Red Star's first piece of major silverware in decades, and I was so proud to help them lift it. Ali was still there at the age of 31. He had gone on to become a Red Star legend and French international.

Was I happy? I was as happy as I could be. I was one of the most famous people in the world, and while I indulged myself in the fame and limelight, I also did my best to use it for good. I tried to represent Algeria as well as I possibly could to the wider audience. I traveled the world, donating millions of dollars. I told the kids who looked up to me that I was not special: I worked hard, believed in myself, and got lucky. I told them that they could be me one day, and I truly believed it because I really was once in their shoes. I wanted to be an idol for them to look up to and emulate. That brought me a very pure and unique sense of joy that cannot be replicated by anything else.

We qualified for the 2030 World Cup, which was set to be hosted in France. I had never gotten the chance to play in a World Cup, and was filled to the brim with excitement. Every footballer wants to play in a World Cup. When it is on, the entire globe stops what they're doing and tunes into the unparalleled, legendary tournament.

We were drawn into the group of death with the United States, Holland and Germany. Most bookies didn't reckon we would make it out, but we were confident of our chances. Some papers were choosing us as dark horses, and we racked up momentum from those comments. We beat Portugal and Uruguay in friendlies leading up to the competition and were as confident as ever.

All of France was under World Cup fever in the buildup to our opening match against the United States. Two of my former Sounders teammates were in the starting lineup for the Americans. I was excited to square off against them.

Algeria last faced the United States in the 2010 World Cup, a match in which American legend Landon Donovan scored a goal in the dying seconds of the match to send the Americans through. It was heartbreak for my grandfather and I, and I was ready for revenge.

The U.S took the lead early on through star midfielder Caden Clark, but we remained calm and kept plugging away. Midfielder Sami Meziani leveled the scores on the half hour mark, before I thumped a volley into the side netting of the American goal with five minutes remaining in the half to give us the lead. The match was essentially a home game for us, as it was taking place in France. The stands were a distinct shade of mint green, and by the time we took the lead, not a word of English could be heard.Former Paradou winger Adem Zorgane wrapped things up in the 81st minute with a delightful chip over the American goalkeeper. We started our World Cup in emphatic fashion.

Mrs. and Mr. Wilson gave me a call after the match to jokingly tell me about their disappointment at me for beating their home nation! They were in their 70's and were still full of life and happiness. Scarlett and I spoke with them nearly every day.
Our second match was a 0-0 draw against Holland. Holland were one of the favorites for the title, and we were satisfied with the result.

As fate would have it, we would have to avoid defeat against the Germans in order to qualify for the last 16 alongside the Dutch. The Germans were favorites, but we had upset the odds before. We had karma on our side, and we knew we had to make up for the injustice of 1982 nearly 50 years later.

The Germans took the lead through an incredible individual goal by Turkish-German superstar Okan Özcan. It would be a glorification of past events to say there wasn't an extremely hopeless feeling around the stadium as the Germans dominated the remainder of the first half.

The Germans continued to dictate play going into the closing stages of the match, however, goalkeeper Samir was having an incredible display in our net, saving shot after shot. Eventually, left back Yasser Larouci was able to launch a lob ball to me on the opposite side of the pitch. The truth was that I was totally off the pace on the day and was struggling to find belief in myself. However, in a flash, it all changed. I one-two'd my way into the German box with Ismaël Bennacer and hit a voluptuous shot into the back of the net. It was entirely against the run of play, but none of us cared.

I was subbed off after the goal in an effort to preserve my legs and defend our advantage. I slowly walked off the field, clapping to the fans and wasting as much time as I possibly could. I saw my grandfather, Scarlett, the crew, their wives and their children smiling at me in the V.I.P. box. I gave them my now iconic wink.

With only a few minutes remaining in the match, Germany were doing everything they could to spoil our day and snatch a winner. Okan Özcan slipped a perfect through ball through to German striker Kofi Adjin, who was breaking away towards goal at a rapid pace. Adjin was a lethal center forward and was unlikely to miss. If he scored, our world cup dream would be over. Just as Adjin was about to strike, our central defender Ilyas Zouabri gave everything he had in his veins to catch up to Adjin and drag him down, making no effort to go for the ball. The referee sprinted over and brandished a red card for Zouabri, meaning that we would play the rest of the match a man down. We clapped him off as he walked off the field. He sacrificed himself to give us a chance at advancing, even if it was slim.

The Germans were to take a penalty kick. If they scored, they would defeat us 2-1 for the third time in World Cup history, and advance at our expense once again.

"It's the same old story", my teammate Mustapha Benrabah sighed out as German forward Lars Gemiti placed the ball on the penalty spot.

Gemiti was arguably the best penalty taker in the world. In his professional career, he had taken 19 penalties. He had made every single one.

I was distraught as I watched on from the bench. It was likely I would never get another chance to play in a World Cup. My eyes began to water. I closed them as Gemiti stepped up to take his kick, expecting to hear German cheers and Algerian tears. Instead, I heard the rattling of the woodwork. Samir had tipped the ball onto the post. Justice for 1982 was to be served. Mustapha and I jumped for joy.

I nervously watched on from the bench as our defence held sturdy and we provided a result that had been in the works for decades. We were through to the round of 16 of the World Cup for the first time in 15 years, and only the second time in our nation's history.

Following the celebrations, I meandered over towards Gemiti, Adjin and Özcan. They were laying on the floor with their hands covering their face. I had played each of them many times throughout my years with Barcelona, Arsenal, and Red Star. I even played with Kofi Adjin in my last year at Arsenal. They were all very honorable men and top-class professionals. I helped them each up off the ground and did my best to console them after their heartbreaking elimination.

"You guys played your hearts out today. You all should be so proud of the way you represented your country. You've all got time to compete in another World Cup in four years. You'll come back even stronger. I know it." I said to them.

"Thank you, Zizou. It means a lot coming from a player and person like you. Good luck in the rest of the tournament."

Okan replied to me. I traded jerseys with him, adding his sweaty, black Germany kit to my illustrious collection that I have conjured up in my years as a professional.

Columbia was our opponent in the round of 16. The togetherness and confidence we had as a group following Samir's heroics against Germany was impossible to replicate. We were ready for whatever the Columbians had to throw at us. Using this momentum, we got off to an electric start. Only 30 seconds in the match, I lasered home a scrappy deflected shot from the edge of the box, giving us the lead in a World Cup knockout game for the first time ever. Forward Amine Gouiri later added to the lead. A consolation goal for the South American's with a few minutes remaining in the match stirred up some nerves, but ultimately led to nothing. We were through to the quarter finals and were the only African side remaining in the competition.

On paper, we were likely the weakest team remaining in the World Cup. However, it would only take three wins to lift the greatest prize in all of sport. I urged my teammates to leave everything on the field in our pre-match meeting ahead of our quarter final class with powerhouse Brazil, the most successful team in World Cup history.

I felt an unimaginable amount of pride walking out onto the pitch. Prior to the kick-off of every match at the international stage, the players on each team sing their nation's national anthem. The words to the Algerian national anthem, "*Qassaman*", were written by Algerian poet and activist Moufdi Zakaria while he was imprisoned by the French during the Revolutionary War. According to Algerian legend, Zakaria did not have access to paper or pencil in prison, and thus printed the words on his cell wall with his own blood. As we sang his lyrics for the first time ever at this stage, I thought about everything I had given to be there. All of the seemingly impossible mountains I had climbed to be on that field. I thought about my community in Barbés, many of whom were in the stadium cheering us on. I thought about my grandparents. I thought about my country. I thought about everyone who had to lose their lives for me to be there; whether that be the millions who died fighting for independence, my own parents, or those the hundreds they murdered. I thought about everything. Tears streamed down my olive cheeks into my scruffy beard as I belted out the words.

> We swear by the lightning that destroys,
> By the streams of generous blood being shed,
> By the bright flags that wave,
> Flying proudly on the high mountains,
> That we are in revolt, whether to live or to die,
> We are determined that Algeria should live,
> So bear witness, bear witness, bear witness!

In the first ten minutes of the match against Brazil, I was having an absolute masterclass performance. Despite the fact that I had scored an impressive three goals in four matches, I had not played up to my usual standard for most of the World Cup. Against Brazil, I felt absolutely unstoppable. I was pulling the strings, and as time went on, I gained more and more momentum. I felt like I was dreaming, and I used it to my advantage. I left my nerves somewhere in my past and dominated the field.

24 minutes in, I received the ball from a Youcef Atal throw in and danced my way past a plethora of players before drilling the ball into the bottom corner in what was likely goal of the tournament. The Stade Velodrome in Marseille exploded in celebration. My teammates and I screamed in delight. We felt ourselves making history.

During the rest of the first half, I played as well as I have in my entire career. The next day, I watched my performance against Brazil back with commentary. The commentator described my performance as 'iconic' as the referee blew the halftime whistle, stating that he hadn't seen such elegance and composure on the pitch since 2006, when a different Zinedine was also playing against Brazil in a World Cup quarter-final.

The score remained 1-0 until the 72nd minute, when I whipped a cross onto the head of Amine Gouiri, and he prodded it past the keeper. The Brazilian players were beginning to lose their composure. Their trademark flair had not been on display in this match.

The match ended 2-0, an upset of extreme proportions, and a result that meant that we would be the first ever African team to compete in the World Cup semi-finals. If we could beat Brazil, we could beat anyone. short minutes separated us from history.

We were to compete against Portugal in the semi-finals, with Argentina facing off against France in the other match. It hadn't been heavily spoken about, but the possibility of an Algeria vs. France final in Paris was on the minds of everyone from both nations.

Portugal opened the scoring in our semi-final through a header by Manchester United striker Luis Carneiro in the twentieth minute. However, we were able to maintain our spirit and rally back. I slotted a finish past into the Spanish net on the brink of halftime, before scoring again in similar circumstances soon after the restart. On the hour mark, my Red Star teammate, Barbés-born 20-year-old Djamel Amara struck a venomous shot into the side netting from twenty yards out. It was his first ever goal for Algeria. The entire team piled on top of him by the corner flag in celebration. We switched to a more defensive formation and fought to defend our lead like the Desert Warriors we were. As the clock continued to tick, we got closer and closer to the World Cup final. I could almost taste it.

Once injury time had passed, Samir launched the ball forward from a goal kick and the referee blew his whistle for the final time. For a brief moment, we went wild in the celebrations. However, we knew we had an even bigger game ahead of us.

Going into the tournament, no one would have expected this Algeria side to be anywhere close to the World Cup Final, but it was a perfect metaphor for my personal rise to the top. Sometimes, things happen. Sometimes, time surprises you. Sometimes, fate, or whatever it may be, manifests itself in miraculous ways.

We watched on the next day as France thrashed Argentina 5-0 to book their place in the final. It was to be a match rooted in history, politics, tragedy and passion. It was to be the most dramatic match in football history. It was to be a war on the football pitch. It was to be a spectacle unlike anything the world had ever seen before.

I tried not to pay attention to what the press was saying in the leadup to the match. I declined all interviews and spent all my time either with the team or with my family and friends at home. The day before the final, I contested a heated FIFA tournament with Wissam, Ibrihim, Sofiane, and Mamadou. Despite the fact that Scarlett and I had recently purchased a mansion near the Eiffel Tower, I insisted that we played in the apartment I had grown up in. As soon as I had the finances, I bought the building and turned it into a community center for struggling youth in Barbés, hoping to keep them off the streets. However, I made sure to keep the unit my grandfather and I grew up in exactly the same as it was when I was a boy. I spent the night in my old room, staring at the same ceiling fan I did when I decided I was going to become a professional soccer player. I wasn't so far from the stars anymore. I reminded myself of everything I had been through. I reminded myself of the boy who watched Kylian Mbappe score in the 2018 World Cup Final with his grandfather and asked himself why it couldn't be him. Twelve years later, I was about to inexplicably get the chance to answer that question.

I fell asleep with Scarlett beside me on the eve of the final. "Guerilla" by Algerian singer Soolking played on the speaker on the desk beside us.

> I sing about love in the middle of this war
> Because I'll always love you, my Algeria
> I sing about love in the middle of this war
> They don't want peace because they don't know about war
> In our heads there's always a war
> In our heads there's always a war

Just as she was about to fall asleep, she whispered in my ear softly. "You can do this. You will do this."

I laid in bed contemplating the weight of the day I had ahead of me. My brain tried to doubt itself, but my heart wouldn't let it. My heart knew I had to be all in. My heart knew I had to believe that I would write history with the same bloodstained pen my parents left me with.

Chapter 18: Le Monde ou Rien: July 15, 2030

Sunday, July 14, 2030 was a warm, summer day in Paris. As the darkness began to set in around the historic city, tensions began to rise. The air grew heavier, and masses began to bite their fingernails. Everyone knew that a World Cup final between Algeria and their former colonizers was not a football match; it was history.

The mood around the locker room was full of nerves. My heart was beating faster than Usain Bolt. I was handed the Bluetooth speaker in the locker room, and put on "Le Monde ou Rien", a hit track by PNL that became the anthem of young Maghrebis in France while most of this squad, including myself, were growing up.

> Anything for my loved ones
> Yeah (x9)
> **The World or Nothing**
> Yeah (x9)
> That's fine with me
> Yeah (x9)

Tonight, it was the world or nothing. Tonight, everything was on the line. Tonight, everything was in our hands; revenge, football, passion, love, fate. Tonight, our slain ancestors would be watching. We were here because of their bravery. Tonight, we would piece time together in a way that history had never seen before.

I felt the grandiose importance of every step as I walked out of the tunnel onto the hallowed Stade de France grass. The sky was fading from blue to black, and the stars were waking up and getting ready to watch the match. The stadium was almost a direct 50/50 split between French fans and Algerian fans. There wasn't a single empty seat in the colosseum, and billions more tuned in from all across the globe. 8 out of our 11 starters were born in France, and 3 of the 11 French starters were of Algerian heritage, with 10 of them possessing African heritage of some sort.

I made *Du'a* before kickoff. I was wearing a black wristband Scarlet had given to me the first day I met her to remind me of her support. I could see her and my grandfather looking down at me from the V.I.P. section. I felt the weight of the green number 10 printed on the back of my white Algerian kit, but I knew I could carry it.

The French attack ran us ragged for the first half an hour. Ali, my teammate from Red Star opened the scoring only 13 minutes into the game with an absolute thunderbolt from 25 yards out. Ten minutes later, superstar forward Jean Monnier doubled their lead with a header from a well taken corner. The French looked to be well on their way to a third World Cup victory.

As I walked off the pitch at half time, I looked out to the disappointed Algerian supporters. It looked as if you had ripped out their hearts and were holding it right in front of them. Nothing hurt more than that. Nothing.

Once our coach had attempted to motivate us, I felt a searing urge to stand up. I gazed out at my teammates and told them that the next 45 minutes would be the most important 45 minutes of the rest of their lives. Sweat dripped down my neck, and fire seared inside my eyes. I would've rather died on that field than watch France lift the World Cup.

"In some alternate timeline, we fold right here and France lifts the World Cup trophy. But right here, right now, we are going to make the decision to come back into this game. We are going to give everything we have in our dense bones. We will play our hearts out. We will win this game because we are meant to win this game."

Some of the players began to nod their heads in agreement.

"For the millions who have died so that we can be here fighting for this crest! For the kids in the broken neighborhoods right outside of this stadium who have tears in their eyes right now."

Many players could barely hold back tears with that comment. I could see themselves feel the nostalgia of their own condition and childhood. I continued.

"For our families, for ourselves, for our nation. We are going to turn our dreams into reality. We are going to do what no one could have ever imagined. We are going to win the World Cup!" I yelled at the top of my lungs.

My teammates got up on their feet and joined in. We all huddled and screamed *"One, Two, Three, Viva l'Algérie!"* in unison before sprinting back out onto the pitch.

There was a shift in momentum going into the second half. I was running the show from the right wing, and my teammates were cutting through the French defense like a hot knife through butter. In the 63rd minute, I received the ball on the right flanked and drilled in a cross with my right foot. Mustapha Benrabah redirected the cross past the outstretched arm of the French goalie. Game on.

We continued to plug away, but by the 89th minute, we still had not been able to equalize despite dominating the entirety of the second half. My greatest dream was slowly but surely turning into my greatest nightmare, and in a few minutes, I would have to wake up. The French were wasting as much time as they could, and with each passing second, our chances of taking the game to extra time dwindled. I looked to the astronomy above me and internally asked for something more. I prayed for our efforts to come good. We were giving everything we had to give. I was as desperate as I had ever been in my entire life.

In injury time, Sami Meziani received the ball just inside the French half. He played a one-two with Djamel Amara before dishing the ball out to me. I knew that this would be our last roll of the dice. I looked up and faked a shot with my right foot before dragging it back onto my left. As soon as I saw the slightest sight at goal, I cannoned the ball and closed my eyes. My heart and the Algerian supporters jumped in unison. Luckily for me, my ears still worked. The stadium absolutely shattered my ear drums, and I roared with them. The shot flew into the net, and the scores were level with the last touch of regulation time. It was a cataclysmic shift in energy. I had put my alarm on snooze. I could dream for thirty minutes longer, and if we won, it was possible that I could dream forever.

Both teams defended with their lives in extra time. No real opportunities were present for either side. No one wanted to take any risks and end up being the player that bottled it for their nation. At the end of the 120 minutes, the match was destined for penalties.

I was to be my team's 5th penalty taker; the penalty that usually decides the shootout.

My soul vibrated with each penalty taken. It took me back to the same anxious fear that Mr. Wilson described my father as having just before activating his suicide vest. That is the best way I can describe the immeasurable levels of anxiety I felt standing at the halfway line.

France scored their first penalty, and we followed it up by converting our first penalty as well. France scored their second, however, Djamel Amara lasered the second penalty off the post. The shootout was in France's hands. I could barely hold in my emotion.

RB Leipzig midfielder Xavier Cabaye stepped up to take France's third penalty and give them a comfortable 3-1 lead. He struck his penalty well, but Samir got his fingertips to it and saved his shot. We were back in it.

Youcef Atal scored our next penalty, and so did the fourth French taker. Yasser Larouci followed coolly finishing our fourth penalty. Juventus winger Theodore Mendy was to take the fifth French penalty. If he was to score, I would be required to make mine or else the shootout would be over and France would win. If he missed, my penalty could be the one to crown Algeria world champions. It was pressure unlike anything I imagined possible in this life.

Mendy calmly stepped up to take his penalty but hit it right down the middle into the grateful grasp of Samir.

I slowly strolled from the halfway line towards the penalty spot. More than half of humanity had their eyes on my steps. I felt the blood oozing through my body. I felt my heart beating out of my chest. I looked up and wondered if they could see me. I knew they could.

There was no doubt in my mind as I stepped up to the ball that I would score. The referee blew the whistle, and I calmly dispatched my penalty into the bottom right corner. As soon as the match ball hit the web-like netting of the goal, tears filled my legendary eyes. I fell to the floor in ecstasy and laid on my back, facing the now pitch black sky. I gave a wink, and I felt millions wink back at me. I was quite literally on top of the world.

When I lifted that elusive World Cup trophy, I felt everything come full circle. I felt all my trauma turn into triumph, I felt hatred turn into contentment, I felt everything fall into place.

After the celebrations, I found my crew. They all had vivid smiles across their faces. I was so proud to call each and every one of them - my best friends. They might not be Algerian, and they might be born in France, but this was a victory for all French citizens of African descent, not just Algerians. This was a victory for everyone who had suffered at the hands of colonization.

Sofiane had tears in his eyes as he found me after the match. After our sweaty embrace, I pulled my wallet out of my bag and showed him the picture he had given me all those years ago of him and my father. He couldn't hold himself together.

"You told me to never forget who I was." I said.

I was choking on my words. He broke down and gave me another hug.

After our coming together, I handed him the photo and sarcastically told him I didn't need it anymore with a chuckle. He cracked up laughing and put it back in my wallet.

As soon as Scarlett spotted me, she sprinted to me with the most wide-eyed smile I had ever seen. None of it would have been possible without her support, without her smile, without her shoulder to lean on. She was my soul mate.

After I had gotten to everyone, I finally approached my grandfather. He was dead silent, with a puddle of tears on the table below him. I approached him and gave him a hug almost as grand as the emotions we were feeling. We didn't share any words. We didn't need to. There was nothing left to say.

We celebrated our victory all throughout the night. Around 3 A.M, once all my loved ones had fallen asleep in the mansion, I arose and put on the custom velvet tracksuit that PUMA had made for me as a special re-creation of the one Sofiane had given me as a boy. The sky was pitch black, but Paris was still awake; in either regret or celebration, depending on where you were.

I walked to the Metro station and hopped on. They were running all night as a special touch from the city for the celebration of the World Cup. I sat down on the nearly empty public transit. It smelled the same as it did when I was a boy. I put on my headphones and listened to "The Egg" by Epic Mountain on repeat. It was a divine production, a work of musical genius. I wanted it to be tied to this memory forever.

After a short ride, I got off in Saint-Denis, not too far from where the stadium I had just played in was. I walked through the streets just like I always had done, completely ignorant of the fact that I had won a World Cup some four hours previous.

I wandered to the entrance of a cemetery I had never been to before. I strolled inside, my phone flashlight lighting up the various tombs. I inched my way towards the back, and found two unmarked, shallow graves. I knew exactly who laid beneath my sore legs.

I tried to open my mouth but couldn't without first weeping. Tears dripped down onto the velvet of my outfit. Finally, I spoke.

"You gave me nothing. You brought me into a world you couldn't even navigate yourselves. You were cowards. You were selfish. You were evil. For so long, I was told that I was destined to lay here next to you. I believed it. You left me in a cruel world. You left me alone," I blurted out mercilessly.

Once I had finally let out my anger, I continued in a less harsh tone.

"You should have received help. You were confused. What you did was unforgivable, but it could have been avoided. Every day, I wake up and wish it was. But now, I stand in front of you a world champion. I spent so long running, and when I finally decided to face the demons you were too weak to confront, I took over the world. I made history, I redefined my name, I wrote a story that will be told as long as there are people alive to hear it. Unfortunately, your story will always be told alongside mine. Two parallels; pure ecstasy and pure insanity."

I turned my direction towards my father.

"I don't deny that I could have been you and you could have been me. I don't think you were born evil. I don't think anyone is born evil. Psychology and genetics are complicated. I wish things could have been different for you. I will never forgive you for what you did to my grandfather. I will never forgive you for what you did to the father of the love of my life. I will never forgive you for what you did to the world and I will never forgive you for what you did to me; but I would give away all my achievements to hear you tell me that you are sorry."

My eyes were full of tears. Each sentence broke as I cried out nearly three decades of trauma. I turned to my mother.

"I don't know you. I don't know your family, and I don't consider you part of mine. I never want to think about you again."

I looked to the sky and prepared my final words for my parents.

"I did what you could never do. I spread peace. I made my grandfather and my nation proud. In my religion, we believe in fate. Maybe this was the way things were meant to be. I owe you nothing, but I hope you saw me out there today. I hope you saw the incredible man I have become without you. I hope you saw me conquer the world without you, and most of all, I hope that you are okay."

I laid the picture of my father and Sofiane on top of his jagged and irrelevant gravestone. I took one last gander at my parents before wandering out of the cemetery and back into the blackness of the night.

As I walked back to the metro, I allowed myself to assimilate into reality. I allowed myself to smile at the incredible life I had lived and couldn't wait to keep on living.

CPSIA information can be obtained
at www.ICGtesting.com
Printed in the USA
LVHW011944231220
674975LV00012B/995